DEMON SLAYER

LINSEY HALL

For A.J., loved always and forever.

M agic's Bend, Oregon
Population: 60,000 Magica, Shifters, and Things That
Go Bump in the Night

"Aeri? Answer me! You better not be dead, or I'll kill you." My sister's voice whispered out of the enchanted charm around my neck.

I slapped my hand to it, muffling the sound.

"Shut it, Mari!" I hissed. "I'm still tracking him."

And this demon was fast. He'd led me on a chase through the city streets all the way to the cemetery entrance. Which was actually quite thoughtful of him. Here, I could kill him without witnesses. I'd have to remember to thank him before I sent him back to the Dark World.

"Aerdeca, you listen to me!" Mari said.

Oh dang, she'd used my full name. That meant she *really* wanted me to pay attention.

"Danger coming from behind. Aethelred says so."

"But the demon is in *front* of me, going through the cemetery gate." My sister's seer friend was never wrong, though. Nerves prickled along my skin as I peeked behind me.

On the other side of the street, a tall shadow moved.

A man?

Maybe, but that was a problem for future Aeri. Right now, I had a demon to catch.

And even if someone were there, he couldn't see me. Not as long as I wore my ghost suit, which made me nearly invisible. The simple white fight suit with a hood and veil made me look like a slight shimmer in the air, and no one knew to look for that.

"Mari?" I whispered. "You gotta be quiet now. I've almost got him."

She grumbled, but I could hear the agreement in her voice.

Just in case, I tapped the comms charm at my neck, lowering the volume, and sprinted toward the cemetery gates. The demon had escaped the Dark World two hours ago. It was my ordained job to catch him, and damned if I'd fail. Especially since he was of the baby-eating variety.

At the cemetery entrance, the heavy wrought-iron gate had swung shut behind the demon. I darted left, scrambling over the stone wall that circled the cemetery. Right before I dropped down on the other side, I caught sight of the shadow I'd seen earlier.

It *was* a man.

Tall and broad shouldered, though I could make out no details in the dark. A shiver of awareness raced over me.

He was headed right toward me, and it sure as heck felt like his gaze was glued to mine.

Shit.

Could he see me?

No way.

Which had to mean he was hunting demons, not me.

I hoped.

I dropped down behind the big stone wall and turned, crouching low to the ground as I surveyed the rows of graves and the mausoleums beyond. Tendrils of fog snaked around the headstones, giving the place a totally haunted feel. Which was accurate, since it actually *was* haunted.

Ahead, the demon slipped behind one of the small white buildings, his body huge and gray. Massive horns rose from his head, and dozens of weapons hung off his leather vest, making him look like a violently decorated Christmas tree.

I darted toward him, drawing my mace from the ether. Depending on the circumstances, I also used a sword or dagger, but I was in a smashing kind of mood today. The heavy spiked ball on a chain would be perfect. The weapon glinted white under the moonlight. The demon stiffened, as if he sensed me nearing, then turned.

His flame-red eyes searched the area around where I stood, finally landing near me. I grinned, knowing he couldn't see me.

"Who's there?" His voice sounded like two huge boulders scraping against each other. He raised a hand that gleamed with blue magic.

I crouched, ready to dodge. He couldn't see exactly where I was, but he was looking in my general direction. At most, he could see the slight shimmer in the air where I stood.

"Who's there?" He sounded even more annoyed.

"Your worst nightmare." I gave it my best Batman impression, grinning.

My sister Mordaca—Mari, to me—would say I should be more cautious, but I needed the challenge. After years as a demon slayer, it was getting to be a bit old hat.

The demon scowled and hurled his blast of blue magic. It flared brightly as it flew through the air, headed straight for me. I dodged, sliding along the damp grass. The magic plowed into a headstone behind me, and the enormous stone structure shattered. I covered my face as the shards of rock pelted me.

A piece sliced my hand, and pain flared.

I looked up, catching sight of the demon hurling one more sonic boom—right at me.

I scrambled away, my hands digging into the damp grass. The magic crashed into my side, slamming me against a headstone. It felt like a punch from a giant fist, and tears smarted my eyes.

I groaned, rolling onto my side. My mace lay next to me.

How had that bastard seen me?

My gaze caught on a long section of grass that looked like it'd been crushed. It had—when I'd slid out of the way of the first sonic boom.

Clever demon.

My favorite kind.

Quickly, before the demon could power up some more magic, I scrambled to my feet and grabbed the chain of my mace, then charged him. My whole body ached, but I ignored it.

By now, I was a pro at that.

The hulking beast stood between two of the small mausoleums, little marble buildings that housed the remains of Darklane's dead.

Instead of approaching head-on, I darted right. There was a series of successively taller tombstones that led to the top of the mausoleum. I sprinted toward them and jumped onto the first, using the other ones like stairs to reach the top of the small building.

Years of practice made my footsteps silent, and by the time the demon looked up, it was too late. I leapt down upon him, swinging my mace for his head.

He moved right before I made contact, and the spikes of the mace dragged against his chest instead of crushing his skull.

He roared, his rage vibrating through me, and swatted at me. A big hand crashed into my arm, shoving me aside.

Damn it.

The demon whirled to face me, yellow eyes searching blindly. Blood poured from the wound at his chest.

I raised my mace and swung for his head.

The steel crashed into the side of his skull. Shock widened his eyes for a fraction of a second, so fast I might have imagined it.

Then his head jerked violently, skull crushed and blood spurting. I grinned and stepped sideways, neatly avoiding the spray. The big demon toppled to the ground, his body slamming into the grass.

Quickly, I stashed my mace in the ether and drew a small glass vial out of my pocket. I yanked the cork out and knelt at the demon's side, pressing the vial to his bleeding neck so it filled up with dark blood.

Once upon a time, I might have been grossed out by the raw flesh and other squishy bits, but that was a *long* time ago. Now, this blood was like gold.

Not only was I a demon slayer, I was a Blood Sorceress. Most of the demons I killed had liquid gold running through their veins. I used this stuff to make spells with my sister, which we sold for a pretty penny. It was our side hustle, and also our camouflage, since no one knew I was a demon slayer except for the council who'd anointed me. It didn't necessarily have to be a secret, but making it one helped us hide from our past.

Once the vial was full, I filled a second. Then I patted down the demon's pockets for charms. Mari and I could make all sorts, but not everything. And demons often carried cool stuff.

I found a transport charm in his right pocket and shoved it into my own. Mari had transporting abilities, but I didn't, so I loved these things.

I checked the demon's last pocket, but found nothing. He was already starting to disappear, his body fading away. If a normal person killed a demon, they'd go back to the hell that they'd come from.

Not me. I was a demon *slayer*. If I killed them, they stayed dead. I was basically a professional murderer, but I definitely didn't feel bad about it. Demons weren't supposed to be on earth —they were inherently evil. Their top hobbies included eating people and murder.

So yeah, not nice.

I finished with the demon and touched the comms charm at my neck. "Hey, Mari? I'm done. Coming home."

"Good. Hurry. Aethelred said trouble is coming."

That damned seer. He was always making predictions about things to come, but they were rarely good. He never told me I was going to win the lottery or a lifetime supply of Cheetos.

I stood, ready to hightail it home.

As if I sensed something, the hair raised on my arms.

I got a hardcore hunted-animal feeling as I turned.

A man stepped out from behind one of the mausoleums, the fog snaking around his ankles.

The shadow that had been following me.

Just looking at him felt like a punch to the gut.

He was even taller than I imagined—probably six and a half feet. His shoulders were broad and his waist narrow. He had the body and stance of some kind of super warrior. Relaxed, but ready to kill.

I recognized it, because I saw it in the mirror every morning. Even his clothes were the kind you could fight in—a battered leather jacket and perfectly cut dark pants that didn't hide the muscles in his thighs.

But his face.

Damn.

He looked like some kind of sexy lumberjack bruiser, with a heavy jaw and dark eyes. A nose that had been broken once but only made him hotter. And his lips.

No. Look away from his lips.

It didn't matter how full they were—I had secrets to keep and this was just the kind of guy to reveal them.

It was impossible to ignore his magic, though. It crashed over me like a tidal wave.

Every supernatural had a magical signature that corresponded to one of the five senses. Generally speaking, good magic smelled or tasted good, whereas dark magic was gross. More powerful supernaturals had more signatures. This guy had all five, and *boy, were they strong.*

I backed away slowly as his magic rolled over me. It smelled of a rainstorm and sounded like the roar of a river. Tasted of aged rum—sweet and spicy at the same time—and looked like an aura of silver moonlight.

But the worst—the worst of all—was how it felt.

Like a shiver at the back of my neck. And not a bad one.

It took only a second to absorb everything about him, but it felt like ages.

Since he couldn't see me, his dark eyes traced over the demon at my feet. His jaw was set in hard lines.

"Damn it." His voice was low and rough, annoyance echoing in the tone.

Then his eyes traveled up, sweeping over the graveyard, no doubt looking for whoever had killed the demon.

They landed on me, and he frowned.

My heart thundered so loudly he could probably use it as a homing beacon to find me.

"That's the trouble," Mari whispered, so quietly I could barely hear her.

And she was *so* right.

This guy was trouble.

I turned and sprinted, racing away. My footsteps were silent on the grass, and I turned back only once to look at him.

His gaze continued to sweep over the cemetery.

Oh, thank fates. There were a few rare supernaturals who could see through my ghost suit. Not him.

I turned left, cutting through the cemetery and leaping over smaller headstones. As I neared the cemetery wall, the air quieted. The man's signature disappeared—I'd left him far enough behind.

"Does he know what I am?" I whispered to the comms charm. "Is that why he's trouble?"

"I don't know. Aethelred doesn't know."

Like all seers, Aethelred couldn't see all. But what he did see was always true.

No matter what, I didn't want this guy knowing what I really was. My big secret.

I have dragon blood.

In theory, I could create new magic—if I was willing to risk it —but that was totally forbidden.

The only person who knew was my sister, Mari, because she had it, too. The world knew us as Mordaca and Aerdeca, the sophisticated, creepy Blood Sorceresses who lived in Darklane.

What they didn't know was that we had a secret life. Even our closest friends didn't know.

I sprinted toward the cemetery wall and leapt over it. My boots slammed onto the damp cobblestones, and I raced down the narrow street. It was bordered on either side by ramshackle wooden houses that were boarded up. As usual, yellow eyes peered out at me.

I waved, unable to help myself despite the fact that my heart was beating a mile a minute. The yellow eyes belonged to city trolls, and they were generally total jerks.

They hissed at me to prove it.

"Love you, too," I said.

Music blared from the pub up ahead. I was almost home. I turned left at the Banshee's Revenge, catching sight of the revelers through the window, and turned on the main avenue that cut through Darklane, the dark magic neighborhood of my town.

Magic's Bend was the largest all-magic city in America, with a population of over sixty thousand. No humans lived here, or even knew it existed. The Great Peace, one of the most amazing pieces of magic ever created, kept us hidden from humans. If they approached Magic's Bend, they'd be compelled to turn back without ever realizing why.

The main street through Darklane was busy at this hour. Here, nighttime was when people really came out to play. Though the rest of Magic's Bend was like a normal city—if you ignored the Fae and shifters and other monsters—this neighborhood was downright creepy. Not everyone here was evil—Mari and I weren't—but a lot of them were *real* iffy.

I slowed so I could easily avoid people, sticking to the edge of the sidewalk, right up against the buildings. I was still invisible, and in the hustle and bustle of the city, no one would notice me. I'd been slipping unnoticed through these streets for years. No one would mess with me if I showed myself, but I just didn't feel like talking to anyone. I rarely did.

Most of the buildings here were three stories tall, built back during the eighteenth and nineteenth centuries. The fancy Victorian architecture and formerly bright paint was now covered with a layer of grime—the remnants of dark magic hanging in the air.

I passed by shops selling all kinds of magic, from potions to shrunken heads, and restaurants where witches made deals over tiny glasses of strong black wine. A dark Fae with gray wings slipped by me, her eyes scanning the area where I walked. As expected, she kept going, unable to see me.

Once she passed, I pressed my fingertips to my comms charm and whispered, "What kind of trouble was that guy back in the cemetery?"

There was a pause, perhaps as Mari talked to Aethelred. Finally, she spoke. "The kind that will change your life forever. And he can't tell if it's in a good way."

Eek.

We'd gotten our life to a really good place—I wanted it to stay that way.

There was really only one thing to do in this situation. Ignore it. I was a champion avoider.

"It doesn't matter," I said. "I'll never see him again."

I swore I could hear Aethelred chuckle in the background and scowled. He said his goodbyes to Mari, and I was grateful. She was the only one I wanted to talk to. Her, and a nice stiff drink.

I picked up the pace and hurried toward my house and shop. It was just up ahead—a once purple building that was now mostly black. A creaky sign hung over the door—*Apothecary's Jungle.*

Ignoring the narrow stairs that led up to the front door, I slipped down the side alley and entered through the back. When invisible, it was never good form to open a door. In a world where invisibility was pretty normal, doors opening on their own were an obvious tell.

Obvious tells would get me killed.

The side alley was dark and quiet as I slipped into the back garden, and then toward the rear of the house. Protection charms prickled against my skin as I touched the doorframe. My magic disengaged the charm and I entered.

As soon as the door shut behind me, my shoulders sagged. I

flicked my hand in front of my face, and the magic faded from my ghost suit. The hood and veil were gone—which I never really felt anyway, since they were made of magic—and I wore regular tactical wear, though it was white. My signature.

It was the outfit I wore to fight battles, but only Mari knew that it could make me invisible. I saved that for my gig as a demon slayer.

Quickly, I strode through the dim corridor, calling out, "Mari! I'm home."

Our house was actually much bigger than it looked from the front. Years ago, we'd bought up the buildings on either side and hollowed them out. I lived on the left and Mari lived on the right. The house in the middle was our workshop and public area. The space where Aerdeca and Mordaca lived—our Blood Sorceress personas.

But it wasn't really a persona. I was just as much a Blood Sorceress as I was a demon slayer.

I strode through the hall toward our workshop, entering the room through the back entrance. A huge wooden table sat in the middle of the space, with a hearth on one of the shorter walls. Bundles of herbs hung from the ceiling, giving the place a lovely floral scent. Tall shelves ran along one side, cluttered full of vials of potions and ingredients. The tools of our trade—mortars and pestles, daggers and crystals—were scattered all over the room.

It was the work that paid the bills. For the right price, we could use our blood sorcery to make charms and spells, performing all kinds of magic that people would pay a hefty amount for.

I dug the two vials of demon blood out of my pocket and set them on the shelf. The people who came to us for spells didn't realize what was in most of them, and I wasn't telling. The demon blood was often our secret ingredient, and it was just a bonus that I could get it through my gig as a slayer.

"Finally!" Mari's smoky voice came from the other entrance. "I was worried."

I turned and grinned at her. "You knew I'd be fine."

She shrugged one slender shoulder that was barely covered by her scandalous black dress. "True enough. You're tough as an old broad with a battle ax. But still, I worry."

"I know." And I loved my sister for it. We were a team of two against the world.

Together, we'd been through thick and thin, heaven and hell. These days were more heavenly, but our past was hell. Which was the main reason that Mari was dressed like a magical version of the vampy Elvira from that old movie.

Her black dress plunged low between her breasts, sweeping the ground in dramatic fashion. Black hair was piled high over her head in a beehive, and a black sweep of makeup surrounded her eyes. She tapped her painted black claws on the doorframe as she inspected me for wounds.

Sometimes Mari really dressed like this—she did like it, after all—and sometimes it was a glamour. Frankly, it was a pain in the ass to do your hair like that every morning, so the glamour was a lifesaver. But no matter what, the outside world saw her only in this getup or her black fight gear.

I had a similar disguise, except white and classy. Ice queen, was how most described it. Though it was a disguise, it was also part of me. I liked my ice queen side.

Our past selves had been scrappy fighters. When we were dressed as Aerdeca and Mordaca, *no one* would guess that the two of us were Aeri and Mari, the two urchins who'd escaped from Grimrealm, determined never to go back. There, we'd been forced by our families to use our magic for evil. Had we not escaped, we'd be dead by now.

So, yeah. No way I was going back.

"Come on," I said. "I need a drink."

"What happened with the guy?" she asked.

"Nothing. It doesn't matter. I won't see him again."

She propped a hand against her hip. "I wouldn't be so sure about that."

My heart thudded. "What?"

"Aethelred said you haven't seen the last of him. And that he's from Grimrealm."

Grimrealm?

Oh, shit.

2

"Now, I really need a drink." I gestured for Mari to follow. "Come on."

She grinned and followed me toward the side entrance to my place. We'd put doors inside the apartments so they connected without us having to go outside. My place was minimalist and serene, though Mari preferred the term *boring*.

I just liked things simple and clean, since it felt like my head was a mess half the time.

The kitchen was all white, like the rest of the apartment, and I headed straight toward the liquor cabinet. Normally, I liked martinis and she liked Manhattans, but I was too beat to mix them up.

"Wine okay with you?" I asked.

"Perfect." She sat in a chair at the little kitchen table, swung her feet up, and propped them by the pile of old crosswords I'd never finished. I didn't have time for them, but I liked to pretend that one day I might.

As if.

I poured the wine into two glasses that I was ninety percent sure were clean, then turned to Mari. She now wore a black silk robe with her hair pulled back in a ponytail. Her face was free of makeup, and she looked tired.

"Glamour today?" I asked. She must have just removed it.

She nodded and rubbed her eyes. "I was too tired to do the hair."

I nodded and sat, handing her a glass. This was the Mari that only I saw. I leaned back in my chair, exhausted. Using magic cost energy, and I was beat. It wasn't an infinite resource, and I needed to rest up to regenerate.

"So, what does Aethelred say about this guy?" I asked.

"Not much, honestly. He was over here for a game of poker when he had the vision. But he's from Grimrealm. Or at least, he has some kind of connection there."

I hadn't met someone from Grimrealm since we'd escaped.

I took a big sip of my wine. "Is he after me?"

"Aethelred didn't know."

I thought about how the big man had cursed at the sight of the demon's body. "Well, he was after me or the demon. I think the demon."

"Bounty hunter?"

I scowled. "Maybe."

"That's your best bet, though. It would mean he's not after you."

"I freakin' hate bounty hunters." I was a demon *slayer*. Slayer. As in, to kill. The bounty hunters wanted to keep the demons alive, at least until they could get their payday. Stupid.

They just made my job harder.

Years ago, when we'd been only teenagers, the Council of Demon Slayers had helped smuggle us out of Grimrealm. They also kept the secret of our origin, and the true nature of our magic and our dragon blood, so that our family could never find us again. It was the perfect deal as far as we were concerned. In exchange, Mari and I became demon slayers, hunting the worst of the worst and protecting Magic's Bend. If a bounty hunter got to the demon before me, then I had to hunt the demon *and* the bounty hunter.

Freaking annoying.

Because no matter what, I didn't lose my prey.

I couldn't afford to. Being a demon slayer wasn't a paycheck —it was a calling. A responsibility. The blood sorcery paid the bills, and the demon slaying was what I did to keep my soul clean.

I sipped the wine, contemplating the guy. Too bad he was so hot. "He didn't see me, at least."

"Good."

"How was business today?"

Mari shrugged. "Fine. Sold a charm and performed a memory spell. Got someone who wants a past life remembrance, though."

She'd need help with that one. "I should be free tomorrow."

I liked past life remembrances. I liked most of the blood sorcery, actually, just as much as I liked demon slaying.

My life was like a coin with two sides, and I needed both to be whole.

Darkness enveloped me, the familiar dream arriving with a bang.

I had no idea how long we'd been in this barrel, but Mari and I had been squished up against each other for so long that my limbs were totally dead and my stomach empty.

The empty stomach was normal, but this was not.

If Aunt and Uncle had realized what torture shoving us in a barrel would be, they might have tried it on us.

Instead, we'd gotten in here on our own, hoping against hope that this escape would be the one that worked. Staying in Grimrealm would kill us, and we'd get out of this underground hellhole no matter what it took.

Mari gripped my hand tight, her breathing fast.

I tightened my grip too. "It's okay."

Could she hear that my words were breathy with fear? That my heart was trying to break its way out of my chest? Mari was normally the strong one, but she was claustrophobic.

So I was trying to be the strong one.

I didn't think it was working.

"When are they coming?" she whispered.

"Soon." Our rescuers were supposed to pick up the barrel and carry us out of Grimrealm. It was the first part of the deal, and if they didn't stick to it, we were screwed. Aunt and Uncle had to be looking for us already, and if they found us before our rescuers...

I shuddered.

Finally, the barrel rocked, then lifted up in the air. Mari tumbled against me. I grunted.

"Quiet in there," a voice muttered from the outside.

I held my breath, smooshed up against Mari.

Hope surged through me, a bright light I hadn't felt in years, as wild terror followed on its heels.

This was it. Our escape.

I gripped Mari's hand tight and shifted so I could peer out of our breathing hole. Flashes of black tents and trade goods passed by, along with the occasional person. I couldn't make out features, but it wouldn't matter. Aunt and Uncle never let us out to meet other people, so there was no one for us to recognize.

Most kids called their aunts something nice like Aunt Judy or Aunt Mary or Aunt Carey. But not us. Ours were just Aunt and Uncle— titles, not names--and I couldn't even be sure we were related.

With any luck, we'd never see them again.

We bounced along in the barrel, every footstep taking us closer. Closer. Closer.

"Where are we?" Mari whispered.

"Near the exit, I think?" I had no idea, but Mari's breathing was getting worse. "We'll be okay."

"Okay, okay, okay," she chanted softly.

Abruptly, we stopped.

"What's in the barrel?" demanded a loud voice.

My heart spiked into my throat. Mari made a low noise.

"Just smoked fish," muttered our rescuer. It sure smelled like it, at least. "Want to check?"

Please don't, please don't, please don't.

We were fifteen, almost adults. If this man found us—he must be some kind of guard or something—would he let us go on our way, or would he send us back to Aunt and Uncle?

He'd send us back—no question. That's why we were in the barrel in the first place. Aunt and Uncle had spies everywhere.

A cold sweat broke out on my skin as we waited, and Mari's breathing was so fast I thought she would pass out.

"No." I could hear the disgust in the man's voice. "Go on."

I squeezed Mari's hand. We're okay.

Our rescuer started walking again. I clung to Mari. We bounced and rattled, and Mari went limp against me.

No, no, no.

I shook her, but she didn't respond.

Terror chilled my skin, and my stomach dropped. No! I couldn't lose Mari. I'd rather die.

I perked my ears for the outside, trying to hear if there was anyone there. Probably not?

I knocked lightly three times on the barrel, our signal for when something was dreadfully wrong. Mari being unconscious—or dead —was definitely wrong. I was so scared I couldn't think straight.

A moment later, the barrel lowered to the ground, and the lid popped off. We tumbled out. I didn't even look up, just shook Mari. Her gaunt face was pale, but she gasped, opening her eyes.

Oh, thank fates.

I hugged her, blood roaring in my head, then looked up at our rescuer. We were in an alley—just brick and stone.

On the surface. Holy fates, we were on the surface.

"We escaped?" I asked.

We had to have. The air was fresher here, the sky sparkling with stars. I squinted at them, awed. I'd never seen the sky before. Just heard stories.

The burly man with messy hair looked down at us. "You've escaped. Ready to live up to your end of the deal?"

I nodded quickly. "Yes."

"Then welcome to your life as a demon slayer."

The alarm blared, a low wail that tore me from sleep.

I scrambled through the blankets, landing on the floor with a thud.

Holy fates holy fates holy fates.

Red alert.

Magic sparked along the ceiling, crimson and bright. I surged to my feet and sprinted for the door, not bothering with clothes. I wore a ratty old T-shirt and a pair of panties with a hole on the butt.

When I was dressed as Aerdeca, I wore silk.

When I was dressed as Aeri, this was as good as it got.

Both were me, but right now, I was the me who had to race down to the enchanted pool and figure out what kind of demon had escaped this time.

Because only the worst demons merited a red alarm.

I met Mari in the back of the main apartment. Her hair was wild and her black robe sloppily tied.

"Red alert." She gasped the words, eyes wide.

It'd been a whole year since the last one, and that alert had been a doozy. A plague demon had escaped, the kind that spread the ancient black death with every footstep.

I had *not* had fun with that guy.

Together, we raced into our workshop. The scent of the herbs hanging from the ceiling normally soothed me—unless there was a red alert.

The hearth was cold and dark, but the hall light shed enough glow that we were able to head straight for the big table in the center of the room. I pressed my hand to one corner of it, while Mari pressed her hand to another. Magic ignited in the air, a faint sparkle of light, and the table levitated, shifting across the floor.

There was a trapdoor beneath, though it was invisible even to us.

Without speaking—this was old hat by now—we walked toward the spot on the floor that was right next to the trapdoor.

I used my sharp thumbnail to pierce my finger. A drop of pearly white blood welled—yeah, that was another weird thing about having dragon blood—and I shook it onto the floor. Mari did the same, shaking off a droplet of ebony blood.

When hers joined mine on the stone, magic snapped in the air, and the floor disappeared. Only our blood would ignite the spell to open the door.

The tiny wounds in our thumbs would heal almost immediately. We used little drops of blood like this all the time, and a while back, we'd enchanted our hands to heal quickly.

I went first, rushing down the narrow spiral staircase. The

stone was cold beneath my bare feet, but I never remembered to buy slippers for emergency occasions like this.

Down here, the earth smelled damp. A pale green glow beckoned us forward, and I raced for it, spiraling downward into the earth. About halfway down, I reached a platform.

Thick green vines snaked across the passageway in front of me, blocking my progress. The aerlig vines were an ancient type of magic, acting as a guard to check the purity of my intentions. One of them reached out and grabbed my arm, squeezing tightly.

"Chill, chill," I said.

The vines were aggressive. If they didn't approve of us, they'd wrap us up until someone came to cut us out. And since Mari and I were the only ones who had access to this place, we'd be here a while. Like, until we were dead.

I pressed my still bleeding finger to one of the thicker vines. There was the briefest hesitation as the plant read my intentions and determined that I wasn't here to do harm. It released my wrist and the rest of the vines parted so I could walk through.

I raced onward, but not fast enough to avoid a slap to the butt by one of the feistier vines.

"Hey!" I shouted back. "Mind your manners."

"It never will." Mari followed me through the vines, and we hurried downward.

The green glow changed to gold as we descended, until we were facing a section of the spiral staircase that was filled with tiny sparkling lights.

Another security measure.

I raced into the Lights of Truth, squinting against the brightness and feeling them brush against my skin, leaving a trail of heat. They froze me in place so I could no longer walk. Voices murmured in my ears, questions filtering through my mind.

Do you mean harm?

Are you evil?

Will you cause destruction?

They'd barely gotten the questions out before I said, "No."

I knew just what they would ask every time, and as usual, they approved of my answer and let me pass. They approved of Mari, too, and she followed close behind.

I hurried through and continued downward, finally reaching the underground chamber that smelled of fresh water and pulsed with magic. A glowing blue pool sat in the middle of the chamber, approximately twenty feet across and the only thing in the whole room. It glittered invitingly, lighting up the whole space.

I raced for it, Mari behind me.

Every demon slayer guarded a Well of Power—this was ours. Not only was it a conduit for our magic, allowing us to perform some mega powerful spells, but it was also a communication device that allowed the Council of Demon Slayers to contact us.

Whenever we brought people down here to perform a spell —a very rare occurrence—we told them that we'd bought the well and property from a witch who wanted to retire to Florida and play Canasta.

I didn't even know what Canasta was.

The truth was that the Council of Demon Slayers had given it to us, along with the house, when we'd agreed to join their mission.

I stepped into the water along with Mari and gripped her hand. Chilly water lapped at my toes as magic swirled in the air.

Together, we chanted, "Here we be, let us see."

The magic that swirled in the air glittered with blue light, moving faster and faster, a windstorm of sparkles that nearly blinded me. The air popped, and the magic disappeared.

Suddenly, a figure rose from the middle of the pool.

Ephemeral and strange, it looked like a cross between a ghost and a person.

I smiled at her. "Hello, Agatha."

Agatha was my contact with the Council of Demon Slayers. She was a rare type of ghost who could travel through the Well of Power, and she was always the one to deliver news of the Big Bads who escaped from the Dark World, a part of the underworld that was so evil that the Council had been created to protect earth from it.

"Aeri. Mari." She nodded at us. "So good of you to dress for the occasion." Agatha eyed my underpants.

I shook my finger at her. "Don't be a perv, Agatha. I know you like my panties, but you'll have to control yourself."

The ghostly figure huffed, and I grinned at her, though I knew the smile didn't reach my eyes. I was too worried about the news she was here to deliver. "What's escaped from the Dark World?"

"A necromancer demon," Agatha said. "One who headed straight for Magic's Bend, though I don't know how long he'll stay."

Shit.

Necromancer demons were exactly what they sounded like. Bastards who tried to raise the dead. Which was so dumb. And dangerous.

"Do we know what his goal is?" I asked.

"No, but he was called out of the Dark World by someone from Grimrealm."

Cold dread snaked down my spine. "So he could know what we are."

"I can guarantee it. But if you kill him, the secret dies with him."

"Wow, way to sweeten the pot, Agatha."

"I thought that would compel you."

"It does." Not that I needed any more compelling. I'd do this because I couldn't let a necromancer demon run around loose. "Where was he spotted last?"

"Assassin's Den. He's big, with gray horns and a green gem in his forehead. He appeared there when he arrived on earth."

The creepy pub was only a few buildings down from us. No wonder that fell within our jurisdiction. Not only did we guard the Well of Power here, it established Magic's Bend as our territory. We protected the city from any Dark World demon that might threaten it.

"Where's his portal?" Mari asked.

Every demon came through a portal, and sometimes they stuck around. We could usually find good clues in those areas.

"Near the business district," Agatha said. "In the tiny alley between the gold building and the Haversham tower."

Mari and I shared a glance.

"I'll take the portal if you want to take the Assassin's Den," she said.

I nodded. We often tag-teamed these jobs this way.

I turned to Agatha. "You can count on him being dead soon."

Mari squeezed my hand.

"Be quick." The energy around Agatha turned darker, more agitated. "This one is up to no good, and he'll be quick about it. Bodies will be rising before you know it."

I shivered slightly.

I couldn't stand zombies. How many would he raise? Were we talking a few ramblers or an all-out zombie army?

With my luck, it'd be the latter.

"I'm on it."

Agatha nodded, then disappeared, her shimmery form sinking back down into the water. I stood in the cold stuff for a second longer, letting the magic seep into my bones. It felt like being wrapped in a warm hug of power, and I'd need all the strength I could get.

I looked at Mari. "Ready to kick some demon ass?"

"Born ready." She grinned. "How did that sound? Legit?"

"So legit."

We turned and hurried up the stone spiral staircase. This time, the Lights of Truth and the aerlig vines gave us no trouble, though the handsy vine reached out and smacked my butt again.

I jumped, annoyed. "You're like an old dude at a retirement home cafeteria, smacking the waitress. Get ahold of yourself!"

"They'll never learn." Mari sighed.

"Nope." I stepped out into our workshop.

A pounding sounded at the door, loud and fierce.

I jumped, looking at Mari. "What time is it? Are we even open yet?"

"It's four p.m. You slept a lot of the day."

I scowled. I was normally a morning person, but late-night demon hunting could really throw me off. "I'll check it."

Since I was still dressed in underwear and a T-shirt, I couldn't open the door. But I loved yelling through it and telling people to take a hike. It was like a favorite hobby.

Before I went to the door, Mari and I touched the corners of the big wooden table. It shifted back into place on the trapdoor. Then I hurried toward the foyer.

"Hold your horses!" As I neared the door, I shivered. The magic that was coming from the other side...

It almost felt familiar.

Powerful. Like a caress. Or a shiver at the back of my neck.

And it smelled of a rainstorm.

My heart thundered as I leaned toward the peephole and looked out.

The handsome, irritating man from last night stared back at me. *The one from Grimrealm.*

He couldn't see through the tiny glass hole, but I could see him.

And damn, did he look good.

It annoyed the shit out of me. "We're closed."

"It's four p.m."

"Still closed." One, I didn't have time for distraction. I had to hunt this demon. Two, I needed to stay away from him.

Aethelred was never wrong, and if this guy was going to be trouble according to him, I needed to keep my distance.

He scowled, his brow creasing in annoyance. "I was told you're the ones to see about a tracking charm."

Tracking charm?

"Tracking what?" I asked.

"Open up."

I scowled, then glanced in the hall mirror to the side of the door. Messy blond hair stuck up all over my head, and my T-shirt was wrinkled. And I wasn't wearing pants.

Yeah, that wouldn't do.

I waved my hand over my face, calling upon the glamour that was second nature to me by now. Magic sparked in the air, and my image transformed. My hair flattened out nicely, forming a sleek waterfall. My skin glowed, and I looked rested and icy.

Most importantly, my clothes changed so my ass was no longer hanging out. A sleek white tank top paired with flowy white pants and heels. Normally I might pair it with a cool white jacket—really working that ice queen angle, natch—but I might be better off showing some skin here. Loosen his tongue a bit.

One might think that my messy fighter girl self was at odds with the calm and cool Aerdeca who was my other half.

They'd be wrong.

Aerdeca was just as much me as Aeri—a stone cold Blood Sorceress who scared people in a different way.

And best of all, no one from our past in Grimrealm would recognize Aerdeca.

I grinned and turned back to the door, swinging it open and propping my hip on it. The corner of my mouth hiked up in what I knew was a sexy smile.

I could have sworn to fates that his jaw dropped a little bit.

"Like what you see, sailor?"

3

A h, shit. Why was I flirting with him?

That was dumb. Normal, but dumb. Often, I jumped before I thought. A lot of times, actually.

I was a sucker for tall dudes with broad shoulders. Even better, this one had the face of a fallen angel who'd spent too much time in a boxing ring. But he was trouble, and I had it from a good source.

"Like it?" His voice rumbled low. "Love it. Very icy."

Well, it was the look I was going for. "Icy? That's your thing?"

"Definitely."

"Well, quit it." I frowned at him. "What are you tracking?"

"I'd rather keep that to myself."

Was it my necromancer demon?

Nah, too much of a coincidence. Just because we had hunted the same one last night didn't mean we'd be doing it again.

I eyed him up and down, getting a better look up. His clothes were definitely nice. Expensive, but subtle. The kind of quality fight wear that I liked for myself. The watch was nice, too. It looked like one of those smart watches that humans wore. That was rare.

Magic and technology were usually pretty compatible, but many supernaturals were old-school. They didn't like to mix with modern tech.

Not this guy, though.

He seemed like the type to take whatever advantage he could get.

And what the heck was his magic? The signatures were all powerful, but none of them dark.

"What are you?" I asked.

"Didn't your mother ever tell you questions like that are rude?"

I shrugged. "Didn't have a mother."

I had an aunt, and she was such a bitch I didn't claim her as my own. She'd kept me and Mari locked up, forcing us to use our dragon blood to create deadly magic. So yeah, she wasn't exactly the milk and cookies sort.

"What are you?" I asked again.

"Interested in taking you out. That's what I am." From the low warmth in his voice, he meant it.

Oh. "Well, that was blunt."

"I'm not one to beat around the bush." He tilted his head, frowning as he studied me. "Don't I recognize you?"

A chill raced down my spine. Besides the moment earlier tonight, I'd never seen this guy before in my life. I'd remember that. He hadn't seen through my ghost suit.

No way.

But did he recognize my magic? I worked hard to keep it under locks, suppressing it so people only felt what I wanted them to feel.

"Are you a dancer down at the Wild Stallion?" I frowned, looking down toward his waist. The Wild Stallion was a male strip club at the edge of town. "Because I go there *a lot*." I tapped my chin. "Though I *swear* I would recognize you."

Instead of blushing or stuttering, he grinned. "You know, I used to headline there. But the ladies were too handsy, so I quit."

"Ah, must have been before my time." I smiled, liking that he kept up with my jokes.

No, Aeri. Get your head in the game.

"About that tracking charm. I heard you were the ones to come to."

"What do you want it for?"

"Afraid I can't say."

"Well, then I'm afraid I can't help you." I was also afraid he was tracking my necromancer demon. That was how my luck worked.

I'd put twenty bucks on him being a bounty hunter—a good one, from the look of his expensive clothes—and I wasn't about to help him. Or get close.

"Good luck." I slammed the door in his face.

"See you later, ice princess." His voice filtered through the door.

"That's ice queen, to you," I shouted.

"I'm good with that."

I swore I could hear a smile in his voice.

I peeked through the peephole. He'd turned around already and was striding down the steps, his movements lithe and graceful. No doubt off to find a tracking potion.

Damn.

There were other places in town to get them. They wouldn't be as good as ours, but they'd work.

"What was that about?" Mari asked.

I turned. She was already dressed in her black fight wear—slim, sturdy black pants and top. Her hair was swept up into a slight bouffant with a heavy ponytail that hung down her back, and the area around her eyes was painted with thick sweeps of black makeup. Mari was even more intense about her alter ego than me, wearing it whenever she might see someone from outside.

It worked in her favor, though. She looked so different with the makeup, hair, and dress. When she wore anything else, no one recognized her.

"That guy from earlier." I frowned. "I think Aethelred was right. This isn't the last I'll see of him."

"Aethelred is always right." She squinted at me. "You like him."

"I don't."

"You do." She grinned. "Your eyes are bright. He's hot, isn't he?"

"Doesn't matter if he is."

Mari pursed her lips and nodded, as if what I was saying made total sense, but she layered it with a nice bit of visual snark.

I scowled at her. "Back to business. Let me know if you learn anything at the portal, okay?" I started toward the back of the house, heading for the door to my apartment. I needed to get changed ASAP and get started. Just the idea of a necromancer roaming around was enough to make my hair stand on end.

"On it," Mari said.

I turned back to her. "Safe hunting."

She smiled. "Safe hunting."

Safe hunting was our thing, and hearing the words warmed me. I gave her one last look and went to my apartment, racing up the stairs to my messy bedroom. The whole place was done up in various shades of white. A dozen different textures gave the place a welcoming feel—knitted blankets, fuzzy pillows, an ornately carved bed, and textured paintings made it interesting.

I dug out my ghost suit—which was self-cleaning, thanks to a damned expensive charm—and tugged it on, following it up with my boots. My weapons were stored in the ether, ready to be pulled out whenever I needed them, and the invisibility hood was already attached to my suit, even though no one could see it. I pulled my hair up in a ponytail that trailed like liquid silver down my back.

I hurried down the stairs and out into the main house. The foyer was empty once again, and I stopped in front of the mirror.

This was a job that called for the ice queen. Mordaca and I were known around town for gathering and selling info. But people were more used to me in the ice queen garb that I'd shown my sexy stalker.

I waved my hand in front of my face to replace my glamour. Once again, I was Aerdeca. Icy, classy, and wearing a sleek white jacket that looked killer. My heels were four inches and so pointy I could kick a demon in the heart and kill him.

It was easy to stride out of the house and move quickly down the street. I might look like I was wearing fancy clothes and impractical shoes—if one ignored their ability to murder a demon, which I considered *very* practical—but since I was actually wearing my fight wear under the glamour, I could move as quickly as anyone.

It was a great disguise. If someone didn't already know me, they were likely to underestimate me.

I liked it that way. The looks of surprise when I beat the hell out of my detractors were priceless.

Since it was winter, the air was brisk and the sky dark already. Clouds hung low over Darklane, which they often did. It was like the dark magic in the air invited shitty weather.

There were nicer parts of town—the Historic District and Factory Row being two of my faves—but Darklane would always be home.

I made my way quickly over the slick cobblestone street. It was a remnant of the past from a place that didn't want to change. Pale orange light shined from gas lamps that looked like they were straight out of Dickens.

I kept my senses alert as I walked, scanning the street on either side. There were people out—five p.m. was a semi-reasonable hour here—but there weren't many. It'd be bustling later tonight, though.

I shivered.

I swore I could feel eyes on me.

Was that guy following me?

I glanced behind me, but spotted no one.

"Sausages! Get your sausages!" The voice echoed from the alley to my right, and I glanced over.

As expected, I saw the sorta-crazy eyes of the sausage man. A sign floated above his head—*Sausages for Sale*—and he wore a portable grill slung over his front. He was an institution here in Darklane, a scammer who sold fake sausages and siphoned off some of your magic when you handed him the money.

He grinned as he saw me and held up a hotdog. "Want a sausage?"

Slowly, the hotdog drooped.

I stifled a laugh. "You might want to consider some Viagra, sausage-dude. That's a limp-looking wiener you have there."

His face fell.

I continued on, leaving him to deal with his sausage.

The Assassin's Brew pub wasn't far from my house. The building had once been blue, but like all the other places in Darklane, it was now coated in the black soot of dark magic. The 'A' in the sign was made of two daggers, but one had fallen loose and hung straight down.

I climbed the steps to the door and slipped inside the old-style pub. With lots of wood and only a few taps for beer, the Assassin's Brew had been there for centuries. Tiny tables were squished together, and there were a half dozen seats at the bar.

As I stalked toward the bar, a few men tried to get my attention. None of them were my friends—surprisingly, most of my friends didn't even live in Darklane. These guys fell into two categories. Some were the users—the dark magic practitioners who did creepy things and wanted to use my magic to help them do those things. The others just wanted me to suck their dicks.

Sweethearts were too dense to know I'd just bite them off.

Flirting was dead in Darklane.

But that was the nice thing about the Aerdeca side of me.

She didn't give a shit. She was a stone-cold bitch, and it was *delightful.*

I found a seat at the bar and smiled at the bartender, a woman who I actually did like. Ruth was a beautiful leopard shifter. She made a great martini and kept her bar in line with a quick wit that she backed up with a mean right hook. If you really got her pissed, she'd shift and bite your leg off.

I respected that about her.

She leaned on the bar and smiled. "What'll it be, Aerdeca?"

"Usual, please. And is Simon here?" Simon was my favorite mole. He had all kinds of intel, and he wasn't the worst. Sure, he was a little slimy, but I could deal with that.

She nodded toward the bathrooms. "Just went to the toilet. He'll be back soon."

"Thanks." I turned to watch the crowd as she whipped up my drink.

A few people were playing cards, and a few were looking at me. I glared at them, and they turned away.

"Here you go, on the house." Ruth set the martini on the bar.

I smiled at her. "Thanks."

I'd saved her brother once. He'd been bitten by an Arachnara demon—basically a giant spider demon. He would've been dead as a doornail if I hadn't gotten lucky and had the ingredients on hand. Neither of them had the money to pay for the cure, but what was I going to do? Let him die? I was pretty cutthroat about getting paid normally, but letting some kid die of super spider poison was not on my to-do list.

Ever since, my drinks were on the house.

It was a win-win, really. And good, because I wouldn't be drinking this one anyway. My signature drink was a gin martini. Pretty much just a cup of booze. But that was the last thing I needed before I set off to hunt a freaking necromancer demon.

I had a role to play, though, and that included a drink. So I raised it to my lips and faked a sip, running my eyes over the crowd.

I couldn't help the feeling of anticipation that shivered along my veins.

He's nearby.

The sexy fallen-angel-boxer bounty hunter dude was nearby.

I could freaking *feel* him. And it annoyed the shit out of me.

Made me nervous, too.

That wasn't something I was used to feeling. And it was irritating as hell.

I tapped my fingers on the bar, keeping my gaze alert on the pub. Though I could feel my sexy stalker's magic, I couldn't see him.

"Aerdeca?" Simon's voice sounded from behind me, and I turned. He was a short guy with pale hair and big ears. Fortunately, he heard a lot through those ears, and I hoped he'd have something good for me.

"Simon. How are you?" I set my drink on the bar.

"Fine. What are you looking for?"

I also liked how he got right to the point. No wasted time with Simon. "A necromancy demon has supposedly come through here. I'm looking for him."

Simon nodded as if he'd been expecting this. He knew I

hunted demons, but he thought I did it for my shop. Their blood was so useful, after all. And it was true—I *did* hunt them for my shop.

I just also did it as a slayer.

It was the perfect cover.

"One of them came through here a few hours ago. Asking about some Merilorca root."

"Merilorca root?" I hadn't heard of that before, and I'd heard of almost all the magical ingredients.

Simon shrugged. "Something rare, I guess. I heard someone direct him to Snakerton."

Of course. Snakerton dealt in the most dangerous and deadly ingredients.

I freaking hated Snakerton.

Not because of the ingredients—I dealt in some deadly shit myself. No, I hated Snakerton because he sucked.

The door to the pub opened, bringing with it a cold whiff of air. I looked over, my heart thundering when I spotted the hot, dangerous guy.

Yep. That damned Aethelred was never wrong.

I shifted so I was hidden behind Simon. "You ever seen that guy before?"

"Declan O'Shea?" Simon nodded. "Bounty hunter. Best of them all."

I nearly cursed. Freaking bounty hunter. Just as I'd suspected.

"Best of," I muttered. Just a bunch of bag-em-and-tag-em losers.

"Oh yeah, best." Simon nodded, eyes glinting with excitement. "He takes only the most dangerous and deadly jobs. Rich as Midas because of it. People say he likes the danger."

Of *course* he did. "What type of supernatural is he?"

"A fallen angel."

"Are you freaking kidding me?" I'd been joking when I'd called him a fallen angel. They were rare as hell and mega-powerful. I'd never even met one before.

Of course he was, though. That was just my luck.

It was time for me to get the hell out of there. There was no doubt Declan was hunting my prey, and I wasn't going to let him beat me.

"Thanks, Simon." I caught the bartender's eye and nodded, then slipped off the bar stool and out the back. I moved quickly and quietly, hoping that Declan wouldn't notice me.

How the heck was he always on my tail?

I didn't like anyone getting too close.

The night was cold as I entered the alley. It smelled of dark magic and pee, a really awful combo. I breathed lightly through my mouth, wishing I could slip into my ghost suit.

Not yet, though.

Snakerton knew me as Aerdeca, and he was definitely scared of me. That was the only form I would show him.

I moved quickly out of the alley, hurrying toward the main road. It was busier now, as the night owls of Darklane came out for the evening. A few old cars were out, and I cut in front of one as I headed for the other side of the street.

Snakerton lived down Blackburn Alley, which was by far the creepiest part of Darklane. The road was only about six feet across, and no cars were allowed. I entered the alley, ignoring the shops on either side that sold all kinds of iffy shit. Shrunken heads and spells made from really dark magic. The kind that were crafted from stolen magic and misery.

Like the rest of Darklane, the buildings were three stories high. The second and third hung out farther than the ones below, creating a tunnel-like effect.

A few people stepped out of their buildings to greet me, but I ignored them. Some of them thought I was as evil as they were. I wasn't. Sure, I had my faults. But most of what I did was in service of guarding this town from demons. It meant getting chummy with these folks sometimes, but if I didn't have to, I wouldn't.

Finally, I reached The Snake Pit, Snakerton's little den of horrors. I opened the door that jingled with an annoying little bell and stepped into the clutter. A purple haze filled the shop, and it reeked of herbs.

I hadn't been there in years, and I didn't regret it.

Shelves lined the walls, each stuffed full of various potions, ingredients, and magical devices. A few waist-high glass cases filled the middle of the shop, proudly displaying wares that made me cringe a bit. Small mummified demons and the like. Not my style.

"Oh, Snakerton!" I called out.

"You!" An irate voice cut through the shop right before something hurtled through the air, headed straight at my face.

4

Instinct made me dive left, right behind the small case in the center of the room.

Shit. He was probably still annoyed that I'd stolen his stash of Garotid demon blood a few years ago.

"Is that any way to greet an old friend?" I peeped out from behind the case, spotting Snakerton standing next to the main counter where he rang up purchases.

His dark eyes blazed with rage, and his villain mustache trembled.

Oh yeah, the little guy was pissed.

Snakerton was small and thin, his dark hair done up in complicated waves that really suited his curlicue mustache. He wore a wild red jacket that looked like it was decorated with giant lizards. Silk pants completed the look. Unfortunately for him, the whole effect made him look like a snake-oil salesman or cartoon villain, and I nearly giggled.

Hell, I couldn't help myself when faced with him.

"I'm sure we can work this out, Snakerton," I said.

"Hag!"

"Hey!" I frowned. "Come on, we can be friends."

Okay, that was an outright lie.

He could tell, too, because he hurled another potion bomb right at my head. I ducked back behind the edge of the counter, which exploded into tiny shards of wood.

Yeah, this was going about as well as I'd expected.

I turned around to inspect the shelving that shielded me from Snakerton. There were about a dozen colorful potion bombs in glass vials, each displayed on a little stand. Because potion making was such an individual art, there was no way to determine what these were. I might put my stunner potions into blue glass jars, while he preferred yellow.

I grabbed a red one, figuring it looked threatening, and popped up, hurling it at him.

The glass flew through the air, glinting brightly. Snakerton's eyes widened, and he dived left, barely avoiding the bomb. It smashed into the shelves behind him, hissing and spitting as it ate away at the wood.

Ohhhh, acid bomb. Nice.

Except now I'd destroyed a bunch of his stock, and he was sure to be even more pissed.

I grabbed a blue bomb instead, creeping around the edge of the counter. I lobbed it toward him. He dived again—fast little bugger—and when the glass exploded against the ground, a hive of angry pixies burst up from it.

They swarmed him, biting and clawing. He shrieked, sounding like an enraged rodent, and I stifled a laugh.

Then the pixies came for me. Four of the little bastards— each a bright pink and blue—dived for my face. I flung my arms up, smacking them away.

"Begone, you devils!" Snakerton shouted.

I peeked out from behind my arms. The pixies poofed into dust. Only the creator of the pixie bomb could command them to leave, but it was a nice safety net.

"There's no need to fight," I said. "I just have a question."

"And I have a burning desire to kill you."

"Are you sure that's not a problem with your diet?" I asked. "You shouldn't be eating such spicy foods. Unless it burns when you pee? Because *that's* a problem I can't help you with."

He hissed and hurled another potion bomb. I scrambled out of the way, but was too slow. It smashed into my arm. Pain flared, an agony that felt like my muscle was tearing away from my bones.

I looked down, horrified to see that my arm had turned silvery and weird. Flat, almost. And it was covered in scales. I raised my hand. But there was no more hand. Just a fish's head.

"You bastard!" He'd turned my arm into a fish!

And it stank.

I darted out from behind the counter, charging him.

He wasn't expecting the direct attack, and I was able to leap on him and throw him to the ground. I straddled him and began beating him with my fish arm, smacking the thing against his face. He sputtered and shrieked.

"Turn it back!" I shouted, nailing him hard in the ear.

"Fine, fine!"

Snakerton was only tough when he was throwing potion bombs. If you got ahold of him, he was a weenie.

"Now!" I smacked him with my fish arm again.

Holy fates, if anyone saw me like this, my rep would be ruined. All those years of instilling fear and awe and respect —boom, gone.

Fish girl.

The idea chilled me to my bones.

Snakerton could be a clever bastard when he wanted to.

He began to mutter under his breath, a spell that I recognized as a common counter curse. Only he could use it effectively since he'd made the spell. Thank fates that the bomb had only hit my arm. Had it hit my chest or head, I'd be up shit creek without a paddle. Hell, I'd be the fish *in* shit creek.

My arm tingled, finally turning back to normal. I wiggled my fingers as I kept a grip on Snakerton's collar with my other hand.

He scowled up at me, his mustache quivering with rage.

Yeah, this dude wasn't going to be helpful. Not in this state, at least. I looked at the shelf above him, inspecting the contents. A vial of pearly white liquid caught my eye, and I grinned.

Truth serum.

I grabbed it.

"Hey!" He tried to hit me, but I smacked his hand away. "You have to pay for that."

"I will." And I really would. Snakerton was a fellow professional, as much as I might dislike him. "But first, you have to take this."

"So you have the ethics to pay for it, but you'll force me to drink it?" He sputtered, turning red.

I nodded. "Yeah, they're a bit wonky. But they're my ethics, and I love 'em."

His mouth dropped open, and I took the opportunity to flick the top off the vial of truth serum and dump it down his throat.

I slammed his jaw shut and pinched his nose. "That's a good Snaky. Now take your meds. They might improve your disposition."

He sputtered harder, shaking his head.

"You're right. You'll always be a miserable bastard. Now tell me where the necromancer demon went."

"No."

I shook him, waiting for the potion to take effect. From the pearly look of it, I was pretty sure what qualities it possessed. Soon, he'd be compelled to tell me what I wanted to know. The words would just burst out of him.

And they did.

"He's gone to the docks," Snakerton spat.

"What docks?"

"The docks at the edge of town. Duh."

"What's he want there?"

"He's catching a ferry to Supernalito."

"Why?"

"You can't transport in, that's why. It's magically protected."

"I know that. Why is he going to Supernalito?" It was a settlement of houseboats built in an oceanfront valley in California. But what did he want there?

"Don't know."

That was the truth, unfortunately. Dang. "Why did he come here? What did he want from you?"

He pursed his lips, his face turning red.

I gave him a little shake. "Come on, spit it out."

The truth serum forced him to speak. "I gave him Merilorca root."

Just as Simon had reported. "Anything else?"

"A bit of Velochia blood."

Hmm, that was weird. "What do those two do together?"

Odds were good my necromancer demon wanted to raise the dead. But *which* dead and *how many* dead had a lot to do with the ingredients he had for his operation.

"I don't know."

Damn it, that was true, too.

"Fine. Thanks for your time, Snakerton." I stood and reached into my pocket, pulling out a few bills to cover the cost of the truth serum.

Snakerton staggered to his feet, sputtering as he adjusted his horrendous red coat. He waved his arms wildly, gesturing to the room. "That's not enough for all this chaos!"

"This?" I turned around to inspect the smashed potions and

damaged shelving. Yeah, I was glad this wasn't my shop. "Collateral damage. After all, you started it."

I pricked my fingertip with my sharp thumbnail, making blood well. Silently, I murmured the words, "Forget of me, I will of thee."

I felt magic swirl around my finger, a combination of my blood and the chant. I raised my fingertip, lunging for Snakerton, and swiped a white streak of blood over his forehead. Then I whispered my curse one more time, to seal it. "Forget of me, I will of thee."

His eyes blurred and his jaw slackened. The swipe of blood on his head disappeared.

Yep, that had worked. He wouldn't remember the last ten minutes, not since the moment he'd first seen me. He'd be confused about the money on his counter and the destruction to his shop, but he wouldn't remember me.

And that was key.

Because this was the blood magic that I wasn't supposed to use. The gift from the dragon that I'd never met. Normal blood sorcery used other ingredients and created spells and charms that people were familiar with. What I'd done here was create *new* magic for myself using just my blood and my words.

I walked a fine line when I did that. As long as I kept it small and temporary—a one-time-use forgetfulness spell instead of giving myself the permanent power of memory alteration—no one would notice, and it wouldn't change my magical signature. It was safe.

Safe-ish.

The thing that Mari and I *never* did was give ourselves new, permanent powers. If I wanted to, I could give myself the power to make gold or kill millions with a single lightning strike. Theoretically, nothing was impossible for us. But it took a hell of a lot more energy and blood. And as a result of our new gifts, our magical signatures would grow.

More magic equaled a stronger signature, like working up a sweat in the gym equaled a stronger stink.

I didn't want to stink.

Especially since it would allow my family to find me. They wanted nothing more than to use me and Mari to create horrible magic. We'd almost died trying to escape them, and we'd never go back.

Never.

I turned to leave, keeping my gaze on the mirror in front of me. It allowed me to watch him as I walked away. He continued to stare into space. The trance would break when I was finally out of his sight.

I slipped out onto the street and headed toward the docks.

The docks were in a quiet part of town, especially at this hour. Darklane might be bustling, but fishermen didn't want to be out on the sea at night. Not normally, at least. That was when the monsters came out.

The cool breeze carried the scent of the ocean, and I sucked in a deep breath. I loved the sea, though there was no reason for it. Grimrealm was underground—no water for miles. So I certainly hadn't grown up with it.

Though maybe that was the point. I *liked* the fact that it wasn't anything like Grimrealm.

No one was looking, so I slipped into the shadows and removed my glamour. My white fight suit was made of a tough material that stood up to scrapes and small blades. The hood that made me invisible would appear when I called on it, though I wouldn't need it now. Anyway, it was normal for me to be out hunting demons in this outfit. When people saw me doing it, they assumed I was hunting for my shop. It was the invisibility and demon slaying for the Council that were the secrets.

I moved back onto the docks and searched for a boat with any activity on deck. There was one on the far end, a ferry about a hundred feet long with two stories built over the deck.

Bingo.

But would my demon prey be on there?

Somehow, I doubted it.

No way he'd arrive super early at a ferry and then just sit there, waiting patiently for me.

I approached, spotting the captain quickly. She was young, a red-haired woman who couldn't be more than twenty-two. But she wore one of those goofy captain's hats and a big badge that said Captain, so I had to assume it was her.

She stood near the side of the boat, and I stopped in front of her.

"Hi. You the captain?"

She grinned. "How'd you know?"

"Your air of authority." *Definitely not the big hat and badge.*

"Excellent. You want a ride out to Supernalito? We leave in ten minutes."

"You read my mind. Any demons on board?"

She gasped. "I would *never*."

"Hmm. Sure, sure." Demons shouldn't be on earth, so transporting them was illegal. "I'm not with the Order of the Magica, so I don't care. Just curious."

The Order of the Magica was one of the two main supernatural governments on earth. They oversaw all magic individuals who *used* magic. Blood Sorceresses like myself, along with mages, witches, Fae, etc. The Alpha Council oversaw the shifters —those who actually *were* magic.

But it was the Order of the Magica who had a real stick up

their butts about rule following. I didn't like them any more than the captain here did. Especially since they'd frown on my true species. And that frowning often led to throwing in jail. Hiding my true nature protected me from them as well as from my family.

"I wouldn't care if you were with the Order." She shook her hair back over her head as if to prove she didn't give a shit.

"Well, I'm not. I'm just trying to catch a really mean demon."

"Bounty hunter?"

"Yeah." The words almost stuck in my throat, given how much I hated bounty hunters. But it was easier to say that than demon slayer, since those were rare, and I didn't want anyone knowing about that part of my life. Because the Council of Demon Slayers had helped us escape Grimrealm—and my family might very well know that—it would be a clue that led back to my true past. No thanks.

"So, no demon on board?" I tried one more time.

"No." She was telling the truth. I was pretty good at spotting a liar, and this chick was genuine. "But another ferry left a couple hours ago. He could have been on that one."

I'd bet big bucks he was.

"Okay, thanks. I'll take a ticket." I tugged the bills out of my pocket and paid her.

She shoved them in her jacket and hiked a thumb toward the second story of the ferry. "You've got berth eight if you want to catch a few Zs. It'll take about five hours to get to Supernalito."

"Thanks." I climbed on board, finding myself a secluded spot at the front. The boat was a lot bigger than I'd realized, probably since we were headed into dangerous waters.

I kept my footsteps silent as I explored the ship, starting at the main deck. If that stupid sexy bounty hunter were here, I wanted to know about it.

And throw him overboard.

The deck was quiet though. Not another soul on board. No wonder the captain had been quick to take my money.

I found some stairs down into the hull next, which appeared to be the captain's quarters along with the machinery. I was no boat expert, but from the size of the engine and all the giant metal bits, this thing looked like it could be fast.

It was quick work to explore the two top decks. They were nothing but hallways with little doors leading into tiny state-rooms. I didn't dare open them. Busting in on another passenger was a quick way to get booted off the boat.

Anyway, my new nemesis's magic was powerful enough that I'd probably sense him if he were here. He wasn't.

I went back to the main deck. Ten minutes had to be almost up. We'd take off soon.

The captain was climbing back onto the boat when I found her.

"Want any help with the ropes?" I asked. "I can untie us."

"Ready to get to Supernalito?"

Ready to leave the sexy bounty hunter behind, more like. I just nodded. "Yep."

"Fine, thanks. Untie the front lines first, then the back." She strode toward the little room at the front of the boat that contained the steering wheel.

I hopped off the boat and started at the front, untying the rope and tossing it on board. The engine roared to life as I made my way to the back, removing that rope as well. I jumped onto the boat and hauled myself over the railing.

I grinned.

Job well done.

I was on my way to Supernalito, and the sexy bounty hunter was still stuck in Magic's Bend. At this rate, I'd beat him to the demon faster than a hell hound ate a steak.

I brushed my hands off and turned to watch Magic's Bend disappear.

My gaze caught on a figure racing toward the boat. Strong, tall, handsome as the devil himself.

Damn it.

I scowled at him.

The boat was pulling away from the dock. We were six feet away. Eight. Ten.

He wouldn't make it. And if he did, I didn't want to be standing here as his welcome party, ready to put a lei around his neck.

Quickly, I retreated toward the bow, finding a shadowed nook to hide in while I watched him approach. Sure, I looked like a creepy stalker, but I was okay with that.

We were twenty feet away by the time he reached the edge of the dock. Even I couldn't jump that. I grinned. This was the part where his shoulders would slump and he'd look all dejected.

Except, it wasn't.

He didn't stop running.

Instead, enormous black wings sprouted from his back. They were tipped with silver, and so beautiful that I gasped. An aura of silver light seemed to surround him, and somehow, he was even more gorgeous.

Ah, shit.

Fallen angel. Right. Of course the bastard had big, magnificent wings.

He launched himself into the air, flying gracefully toward the boat.

I shoved myself back into the shadows, then scowled, immediately horrified by the fact that I was hiding.

But what the hell. I needed a chance to recover from the sight of him.

He glanced toward me, just briefly, as if he could see me in the shadows. I just barely resisted giving him the finger. I had a tendency to act before I thought, and I was trying to limit that these days.

Maybe it was maturity; maybe it was a self-preservation instinct. Whatever it was, I limited myself to a glare.

The corner of his lips tilted up in a cocky smile, and my stupid heart kicked up a notch.

Dumb heart.

He turned and walked toward the little room where the captain was steering. The bridge, I thought I'd heard it called on TV once.

Well, damn. It looked like my competition was keeping up.

I strode to the back of the boat again and leaned on the rail.

My stomach grumbled, a combo of stress and actual hunger. I called upon the ether and withdrew a mini bag of Cheetos. I had a weakness for junk food, especially in iffy situations, which was something that *no one* would associate with my ice queen side. Neon orange Cheetos were one of my faves, and it cost a pretty penny to store them in the ether like this. Most people just stashed weapons and a few other valuables there, paying a mage for the magic.

I created it myself and found it to be well worth the effort.

I chomped down on the cheesy, crunchy treat, keeping an eye on Magic's Bend as it shrank against the horizon. The buildings of the business district rose tall against the backdrop of the mountains, their lights glittering like diamonds. The rest of the town was pretty low to the ground, and I leaned on the railing as I watched it disappear.

Home.

More home than Grimrealm had ever been.

I shook my head, driving the thought away, and focused on the goal.

Catch the demon. Kill the demon.

Not so hard.

I was about to turn and head to my bunk when a voice caught me. It was low and rough, twining around me like smoke. "Ice queen."

The stupid sexy winged man had found me. And I probably had Cheeto dust on my face.

Fantastic.

I shoved the Cheeto bag back into the ether and licked my lips. There was nothing I could do about my fingertips except hide them. I composed my expression, then turned slowly, raising a brow.

But I didn't speak.

Damn, he still looked good. The wings were gone, but his dark hair was mussed from the breeze and his eyes glittered with appreciation as he looked at me.

I liked it.

No.

He had a connection to Grimrealm. And he was still a bounty hunter. A major no-go.

"I thought I recognized you," he said.

"Can't say the same."

"Sure you do." He grinned, calling my bluff with his smile. His damned fallen angel smile. He was so sexy it annoyed me. "Don't forget my time at the Wild Stallion."

"What the hell are you?" Even though I knew what he was, I didn't want to let that slip until he told me. Nothing worse than being caught as a stalker. Just a minor stalker, but still. Embarrassing.

"Fallen angel." He strode to the railing and leaned his arms against it, looking out at the ocean.

I turned and leaned on the railing, too, my shoulder a good two feet from his. It felt like two inches. "Get kicked out of heaven?"

"Something like that. Not pure enough, I suppose."

Oh, I could guess what he meant by that. Warmth unfurled within me. Especially at the sight of the cocky half smile that seemed to be his signature. But was there something tortured in his gaze? Hard to tell, but I wanted to know more.

Fates, get it together, Aeri.

Many of the world's religions had angels. The reality wasn't too far off of what humans believed, though they didn't represent any one religion specifically. More like the forces of good. Angels were immensely powerful celestial beings that were inherently good. They were basically the counterparts of demons, opposite in every way.

I was itching to find out why he had fallen, but clearly he wasn't going to give details. And I definitely couldn't ask about Grimrealm without sounding weird. He had no idea I knew about that.

"What are you?" he asked.

"You know what I am."

"Blood Sorceress. But why would a Blood Sorceress be going to Supernalito?"

"It's pretty much America's top stop for buying ingredients for potions. You can find anything there." I was pretty sure that was true, at least.

"But that's not why you're going."

"You've got me. I'm meeting my boyfriend."

"Maybe, but I doubt it."

"Vacation, actually."

"Nope. It's a terrible destination."

"Maybe I'm weird." Scratch that, I was definitely weird.

"I think I like that about you."

I warmed a bit, then mentally kicked myself. "You don't know me."

"I know enough."

"Like what?" Nerves skittered along my skin. This guy didn't know me. At least, he didn't know anything important. He didn't know my secrets. He didn't know what I hid from. *Who* I hid from.

"You're hunting the necromancy demon too," he said.

I kept my face motionless. "What necromancy demon?"

And how could he know? Simon wouldn't rat me out. My snitch in the Assassin's Brew was too loyal. And too afraid of me.

"I saw you coming out of Snakerton's. Don't play dumb."

"I was just getting some ingredients. I'm on a buying trip. Restocking the shop."

"Not from the look of his place. It was pretty beat up. And there was an empty vial of truth serum."

Damn, this guy was quick.

I spared him a glance, and he was looking down at me, his expression interested. I looked back at the horizon, but Magic's Bend was gone. There was nothing but darkness with the glitter of the moon on the water.

"You're after the demon."

Snakerton couldn't have told him what I was after, but the fact that I was on this boat, right after visiting the last place the demon had gone, was too much of a coincidence. This guy was smart enough to know that.

I shrugged. It wasn't a huge secret, anyway. There was something about this guy that made me want to play my cards close to my vest, but sometimes the truth—especially a harmless truth—was worth it.

"Yeah, fine. I'm after the demon too. I use their blood in my magic."

He nodded, clearly buying it. He'd already known it, so it was more like he'd wanted me to admit it. To get under my skin.

Well, it was working.

"We can hunt him together," he said. "Before I take him alive, you can have a bit of blood."

"Alive? Why the hell would you take the demon alive?" See, this was what I hated about bounty hunters. The *alive* part of *dead or alive.* It should always be *dead or dead* with demons.

"That's the terms of the deal."

"Demons are evil." Full demons, at least. Half demons were iffy since their other blood could dilute the darkness that came with their demon side. "They should be sent back to their underworld." Or outright killed. "Doing anything else is fool-hardy. What if he escapes?"

"He won't escape. That's why they hired me."

"Who?"

"Confidential. But rest assured, he won't be able to get out and wreak havoc."

"Oh, well that makes me feel a lot better." I added a bit of extra sarcasm to my words and nodded. I was *definitely* going to kill this demon when Declan wasn't looking.

He turned to me and held out his hand. "I'm Declan O'Shea, by the way."

I know. But obviously I didn't say it. *Yeah, I was really interested in you and asked around* was the last message I wanted to send.

I stuck my hand out and gripped his, trying to ignore the shiver of awareness that rushed up my arm, followed by a wave of heat. "I'm Aerdeca."

"Just Aerdeca?"

"Just Aerdeca." I withdrew my hand from his, and was immediately colder.

"Let's work together on this. We'll catch him faster that way."

"I work alone."

"Even though we have the same goal?"

Yeah, we don't. "I work alone."

"Then it's a race?"

"Looks like it."

"Then if I win, you won't get the blood you're after. Take the sure thing. Work with me. It'll be fun." He was so cocky, yet somehow still charming. It should have been impossible.

"You won't win." I was damned certain of that.

"Oh, I will."

Annoying and sexy. Yep, those were the two words to describe him. And I wanted to make out with him.

Gah, I'm an idiot.

I stifled a huff and pushed myself off the railing. "I'm going to bed."

"Want company?" A devilish light glinted in his eyes.

Yeah. "No."

I turned and walked away, vibrating with awareness. Ugh. I needed to get my head in the game.

I hurried away without looking back—points for me—and made my way to cabin eight. It was a tiny space—just a bunk against the wall and a little round porthole. I threw myself onto the bed and winced.

"Like a freaking rock." I rubbed my lower back, then pressed my hand to my comms charm. "Mari? You there?"

"Here." She was breathing fast, almost like she was fighting.

"You okay?"

"Just dealing with...a little..."

"Problem?"

"Demon." There was a distant shriek, and she was back, sounding calmer. "He's dead."

"How's the portal? You find anything out about our necromancer friend?"

"Portal had almost disappeared, but I'm trying to stabilize it to see where it goes. Little problem with a second escaped demon, but I fixed it. How are you?"

"Good, good. But the sexy bounty hunter is here."

"Oh, *is* he?"

"And he's a fallen angel."

"Damn. No wonder he felt so powerful."

"Yeah."

"And he's hunting the necromancer demon."

"Right on the first guess."

"Any idea how you'll beat him?"

"Quick wits." I grinned.

"It's worked before."

"You can do it. Just stay safe."

"I will."

"Oh, and Aeri? Maybe give the guy a chance."

I nearly sputtered. "Wait, what?"

"I can hear in your voice that you like him. You haven't gotten out in ages."

"Gotten out?"

"I was *trying* to be a lady. I mean, get laid. You haven't gotten laid in ages."

"Well, I'm not sleeping with the fallen angel who is a freaking *bounty hunter*. I hate bounty hunters! And he has connections to Grimrealm. Don't forget that."

"I know, I know. But he doesn't need to know where you're from. And maybe he's not the total worst. He didn't seem like the total worst."

"High praise." I scowled. "Safe hunting, okay? I'll see you soon."

"Safe hunting."

I cut the comms charm and squeezed my eyes shut, commanding myself to go to sleep. Unfortunately, my mind was an idiot traitor, and all I could see was Declan, smiling down at me.

Jerk.

5

The dream crept up on me, teeth bared and claws raised. One moment, I was nothing—dreamless in a black sleep. The next, I was a child again. Fourteen, maybe. It had been hard to tell time then, back when we were in Grimrealm.

"Do it," commanded Aunt.

Her face was in shadow, and her voice made me shiver.

My gaze dropped down to Mari, who knelt at her feet. My sister was gaunt and pale, just like me. Shortly after Aunt and Uncle had learned of our dragon blood, they'd figured out that the only way to make us use it was by threatening the other.

This time, it was Mari.

Her black eye was motivation enough.

"Okay, okay! I'll do it." I hated trying to make new magic. It hurt and was really freaking scary.

Aunt shoved Mari toward me. "You too. Both of you—become alchemists. Now."

It was so mundane, but better than the killing power she'd tried to make us learn last week.

That had failed—maybe because I'd made it fail.

Mari knelt across from me, her dark eyes big in her pale face.

"It'll be okay," I whispered. I didn't know if it was true. "Just do what I do."

She nodded, her expression stark.

I drew my fingernail over my wrist, making a long cut. Pain flared, and I winced. White blood began to pour, and horror opened up a hole in my chest.

I'd never seen so much of my blood before.

I drew in a ragged breath and watched.

This had to work.

Mari hesitated, just briefly, then mimicked my motions. She opened one of her veins, making a small noise. Black blood dripped onto the stones.

I sliced my other arm, agony shooting through me. My stomach turned.

To make new magic—real, true magical skill that stayed with us forever—we basically had to die.

My head spun as my blood poured onto the ground, pooling around my knees. It mixed with Mari's, and I reached for her hand, gripping her tight.

Together, we began to pour our magic out of us, along with our blood. I gathered it up from every corner of my body and forced it out of me. It sparkled in the air between us, cocooning us against Aunt's hard stare.

As the magic drifted lower toward the blood that had pooled around us, I envisioned lightning. We needed a weapon, not gold.

I met Mari's eyes and mouthed the word, "Lightning."

Her eyes flared wide, but she nodded once, almost imperceptibly. Then she dropped her gaze to the pool of blood.

We weren't going to give ourselves the permanent power of gold production like Aunt had requested—we were going to give ourselves the power of lightning.

A weapon.

Together, we poured out every bit of magic we had, letting it mingle with the black and white liquid. I envisioned lightning—how it would sound, feel, smell. I squeezed my eyes shut, forcing the vision to become reality.

I began to sway, my head going fuzzy from weakness. Losing all of my magic and my blood made nausea roll inside me. My breathing slowed and my muscles turned weak. I couldn't even raise my arm.

My eyes popped open, and I met Mari's gaze.

She was paler than she'd ever been before, her cheeks hollowed and her eyes stark.

We're dying.

Panic gripped me tight, iron bands around my lungs.

What are we doing? *This was insane.* What if it didn't work? We would *die.*

"Keep going," she whispered. "We can't stop."

But she was right. If we stopped now, we really would die. Forever die. We were too far gone and needed this process to finish. To revive us.

Please work.

We kept going, reaching within our souls to pour the last of our magic out of our bodies, joining it with our blood. It was a gruesome ritual, a confusing one that was part learned and part instinct. The last of my consciousness began to fade, my energy entirely gone.

Death was near.

Or maybe I'm already dead?

I was so woozy it was hard to tell. I had no more energy left. No more strength. I was nothing.

But something happened. The magic changed. Our *magic changed.*

It crackled with energy, bright and fierce, and flowed back into us. Stronger than ever, it flooded my veins, creating new blood, new strength. New magic.

I gasped, agony shooting through every inch of me, lighting me up like a live wire. Death was gone, and I was power. Strength.

Lightning cracked in the distance. Again and again.

We were in Grimrealm, underground. There should be no lightning. Not natural lightning, at least.

It came from me.

From me and Mari.

I dragged my eyes open and met her gaze again. The power of lightning crackled through me—mine now, to use forever. Mari had it too.

My aunt screeched in rage.

She'd realized what we'd done.

Oh shit. *We were in trouble.*

A blaring siren tore me from sleep. I jerked upright, panting. For a moment, I was blind. My heart spiked into my throat.

Gasping, I scrambled out of bed, my boots still on.

Boots still on?

The floor underneath me lurched, sending me careening into the wall that was only a couple feet away.

The boat.

Right. I was on the ferry.

And something was going wrong. Like, mega wrong. The siren was the shrieking, frantic kind that made me think it was saying, "We're sinking! Hope you can swim!"

And the waves...

Holy fates, the waves were enormous. I crashed back into the bunk, only to be thrown up against the wall a moment later.

My door slammed open, light flooding the tiny room.

An enormous figure stood in the open space, backlit so I

couldn't make out the details of his features. But from the sheer size of him, and the breadth of his shoulders, I knew it was the number one pain in my ass—Declan O'Shea.

"Hey, sexy sorceress, you okay?"

"Fine." I managed to get myself upright and cling onto a lighting fixture.

"Problem up above. Come on." He disappeared, leaving my door swinging open.

"Problem up above?" I muttered. "Duh."

I sprinted from the room and down the hall, crashing into the walls every few steps like a freaking pinball. The waves rocked the boat like we were a rubber ducky in the bath of one seriously pissed-off toddler. Thank fates I slept in my boots on missions like these. They were my faves, and I'd hate to lose them if we sank.

The deck was chaos. Water sloshed over the wooden planks, and a red light flashed brightly at the front of the boat. Declan's shadowy figure was leaning into the bridge. I stumbled toward him, clinging to the railing as waves smashed into me, threatening to take me down with them.

"She in there?" I shouted against the rain.

"Of course I am!" shrieked the captain.

I caught a quick look at her through the space at Declan's side. She was wild-eyed, with her captain's hat on the floor and her red curls a crazy halo around her head. She pointed to the far side of the boat. "Go stop that squid!"

Squid?

Declan turned to me, his dark eyes serious. He didn't even speak, just turned and sprinted for the bow, racing around the pilot house.

My muscles kicked into action. I ran after him, my mind repeating the word *squid* over and over.

When I careened around the front of the bridge and finally caught sight of the ocean on the left side of the boat, I nearly stumbled.

An enormous squid rose out of the water, four of its huge tentacles slapping the surface to create giant waves. The thing had to be the size of a ten-story building, with huge horns protruding off its pointed head. Massive fangs hung out of its mouth, and its eyes bulged, shining a brilliant green.

"Octopus!" Declan's wings flared from his back, and his magic surged on the air, bringing with it the scent of a rainstorm and the taste of aged rum.

"Nope, giant squid." I really liked aquariums, and that was no octopus. "See how pointy its head is? Definitely genus Architeuthis." With a bit of dark magic thrown in, because damn, that thing reeked of it.

Declan turned to me, his expression equal parts impressed and incredulous. "Now is the time you're focused on scientific accuracy?"

As if to punctuate his point, the squid slapped a tentacle down right in front of the boat, sending a massive wave crashing over me.

I gripped the railing tight, but it was just too much water, even for my strength. I lost my grip, tearing away from the railing and riding the wave along the deck.

A strong arm grabbed me around the waist, pulling me in toward a warm body that was hard as iron.

My heart leapt into my throat. I blinked water out of my eyes, looking up into Declan's face. "It's always a good time for scientific accuracy. Especially with the mega fauna of the ocean's depths."

He cracked a smile, then laughed.

I pulled away, lunging around him to grab the railing and

look at the squid. Beneath the moonlight, it gleamed silvery green.

And it was closer. Close enough to grab the boat.

"Hold it off!" the captain shouted.

This job called for a sword.

I drew the weapon from the ether, its weight comforting in my hand.

One of the enormous tentacles reached out and wrapped around the front of the boat. I leapt for it, swinging my sword in a downward arc. I gave it my all, imbuing it with every ounce of power I had. My dragon blood gave me extra speed and strength.

The steel sliced right through the tentacle. A poof of black magic burst upward, then black blood went flying. I dived low, skidding on the wet deck. The severed tentacle still hung heavily over the front of the boat. The vessel couldn't bear that much weight and was already dipping downward.

I leapt up and scrambled to the far side of the boat, where the tentacle hung down into the water. I raised my sword and slammed it down, severing the limb so the extreme end splashed into the sea.

Black magic poofed from the wound again, an indicator that this creature wasn't technically living. He was some kind of horrible dark spell that had been cast on the ocean, guarding something or haunting something.

I had no idea which.

At some point, Declan had launched himself into the air. His wings beat powerfully, making the air vibrate, as he swooped low over the squid.

The monster was about to wrap another tentacle around the back of the boat, but Declan hit it with a massive golden lightning bolt. It wasn't white like all the other lightning bolts I'd ever seen.

Nope, that'd be too normal for the fallen angel.

"We're nearly there!" the captain shouted. "Hold him off just a bit longer!"

I turned to look at her through the bridge window. Her eyes were wild as she pointed to the riotous sea ahead. About two hundred yards away, two enormous pillars of stone jutted out of the ocean.

"We just have to make it through there!" she shouted. "It can't follow."

"On it." I turned to face the squid.

Declan was fast, swooping gracefully through the air as he hurled lightning at the monster.

There were no other passengers on board, so it was up to me and him to take out the beast.

Unfortunately for us, it had more than eight tentacles. I'd severed one and Declan had incapacitated at least five. But somehow, there were still another five waving above the surface, slamming into the water and reaching for the boat.

One of them crept behind Declan, rising high above the deck.

We needed to get to the head. That's where we'd take it down.

The tentacle was about to smash us when I got an idea. Quickly, I sliced my finger with my blade.

As the tentacle lowered toward the deck, I took a running leap and jumped onto it, clinging like a monkey.

The tentacle jerked upward, as if the squid were shocked. I still had the sword gripped in my right hand, so I used it to make a tiny cut on the back of the squid's long appendage. Then I pressed my bleeding finger to it, letting our blood mingle together.

Mixing our bloods made the suggestive spell stronger, and there was no way Declan had seen me do this little bit of dragon blood magic.

"Eat me," I said. "You want to eat me."

Like the forgetfulness that I'd compelled Snakerton to feel, I used my blood sorcery and the power of suggestion to get the squid to retract its limb, carrying me toward its mouth.

I flew through the air, the sea disappearing below me as the squid lifted me higher and higher.

"Eat me."

I tightened my grip on the squid as it dangled me over its mouth, looking for the perfect opportunity to jump. In the distance, I could see the angel hurtling toward me, powerful wings carrying him through the air.

Damn it, I didn't want him getting in the way.

Fortunately, my moment came. The squid dangled me right over its eye, and I dropped, my blade pointed downward.

The steel pierced the green eye, and a poof of black magic rose upward. The creature shrieked, pulling back as my blade slipped free. I stashed my sword in the ether, then pushed off of the squid's head with my feet, wanting to plunge into the water away from its body.

My superior strength helped me push off hard, sending me flying gracefully through the air. It was rare I got to fight at sea, but it was one of my all-time faves. I had the perfect swan dive planned when something yanked on me, jerking me to a stop.

The angel.

He'd caught me in midair, gripping me to his strong chest.

For fate's sake.

He'd ruined my perfect aerial descent.

I glared at him as we hovered in the sky. "Damn it, why'd you do that?"

He glared right back at me. "I'm saving you."

"Saving me?" I nearly shrieked the words, pointing back at the squid who was now thrashing in the water, no longer a threat. "Does it look like I need saving? I just took out that squid."

He shrugged, as if conceding my point. "The sea is cold and rough."

I laughed, then elbowed him so hard that he dropped me.

"Hey!" he shouted.

Triumph surged through me as I spun in the air, twisting for the perfect landing. It was the best feeling in the world, soaring through the cold air with the sea beckoning. I wasn't any kind of water creature—I just freaking loved the ocean.

I hit the water as a perfect column, diving deep and then arcing up toward the surface. The ocean welcomed me, warmer than the icy air at the surface, and I kicked for the boat, cutting through the ocean with strong strokes.

The ship was still about fifty yards away, nearly to the pillars of rock, so I picked up the pace, grateful for my strength. It'd be *real* embarrassing if I'd insisted on saving myself then couldn't manage it.

I nearly laughed at the hilarious idea.

As if I couldn't save myself.

I reached the boat and climbed the hull like a bilge rat, an agile creature that was really too maligned. I couldn't help the smile that stretched across my face as I leapt onto the deck.

"You're nuts!" shouted the captain.

Declan landed a half second later, looking at me like I was crazy. "You *like* swimming in that water?"

"Love it." I propped my hands on my hips and grinned back at him, but it was more of a baring of teeth.

In fairness, I normally wouldn't turn down being rescued. I had too good a sense of self-preservation, and I knew my limits. Mostly. But he'd annoyed the hell out of me by trying to swoop in and get the necromancer demon, and I really did like plunging into the sea after using a giant squid's head as a diving board.

Anyway, it was over. The squid had sunk beneath the waves, and the captain was piloting us through the great pillars of rock, out of its territory.

Declan gave me an appraising look. "You're stronger than a normal woman."

"Blood Sorceress, remember?"

"Blood sorcery doesn't normally come with greater strength and speed."

He had a point there. That came from my dragon blood, not from my sorcery. But I had a good answer for that too. "There's no limit to the spells I can create."

Cockiness echoed in my voice, and he grinned, seeming to like it. "Now that, I believe."

His words warmed me, which of course immediately made me freak out. He was supposed to be repelled by my confidence. A lot of dudes were.

Not this one, apparently.

I didn't *want* to like him, damn it. I glared at him, knowing I was being rude and prickly and not caring. "Don't get in my way."

The words rolled off his back like water off a duck's. He just grinned. "We can be a team. We'd make a good one."

He had lightning and wings and speed and strength. Probably a few more things as well. He'd be a good ally.

But I didn't want to work with him. Too risky. I needed to kill this demon before he nabbed him. If Declan didn't play fair and I helped him get to the demon, he could grab him and transport out before I even had a chance to put steel to skin.

"Nah." I shook my head. "I work alone."

He opened his mouth, but I turned away. Honestly, I didn't

want to hang around him long enough to change his mind. Not that I'd do that, but I actually might do that.

I kinda liked him, and I definitely wanted him.

I'd also never been any good with self-control. It was over-rated, as far as I was concerned. Which meant that I had to walk away. Now.

The thing was, I could feel his gaze on me as I left. And I liked it.

6

F ortunately for me, the captain had a magical drying station on board. "So many storms," she said. "And I hate rain jackets."

Whatever her reasons, the thing was saving my butt. It was basically a giant blow dryer, and it got me warm and dry. I could do this job while freezing, but I didn't want to.

When I was done, Declan took my place. The waves had soaked all three of us, but thank fates, they were gone. As he walked into the drying station, I eyed him, unable to keep my gaze off him.

Why had he fallen?

What exactly did he mean by not *pure* enough?

I shouldn't be interested. Nope, no way.

We were approaching Supernalito, which was like a supernatural cousin to Sausalito on the California coast, so I turned my attention toward that. The humans had no idea it was there, of course. The little bay was carved into the mountains on the Pacific side, protected from the sea by the narrow harbor entrance and the great pillars of stone.

The harbor itself was stuffed full of tiny docks that formed a maze, connecting hundreds of houseboats. It was a city built on water, with mountains surrounding it. Golden lights gleamed on the hillside, evidence of buildings climbing their way up to the peaks. There were big patches of black—natural area, I had to assume—and I searched them, wondering where the demon had gone.

"There won't be another ferry back until mid-afternoon," the captain said.

"Thanks." I walked to the railing, making sure to keep far away from Declan, and inspected the town as we neared.

The houseboats were all different colors and shapes. Some looked like cottages, others like boats. Some were even done up in the shapes of animals or shoes.

The damned demon could be *anywhere*.

I tried to be sneaky as I peeked at Declan, who'd joined me on the deck. Did he know where the demon had gone?

He was probably tracking him like me, through Snakerton. Which meant no—he just knew that he was somewhere in Supernalito.

So he probably didn't have a lead on me.

His wings unfurled from his back, and he launched himself into the air, shouting a quick thank you back to the captain.

Damn it!

We were still a good two hundred yards from the nearest dock, and he was going to freaking fly it.

So much for him not having a lead. I crossed my arms and glared at him as he flew off.

Bastard.

I turned to the captain, going to stand in the open door to the bridge as she steered us toward the docks.

"There was a demon on the last boat," I said. "Are there any places in Supernalito where demons are known to congregate?"

It wasn't a given that he'd go find his own kind, but it was a thread I could pull on, at least.

"Not really." The captain shook her head, red curls bouncing. "But since you're looking for one in particular, I'd speak to Florence. She sees everything."

"Who is Florence?"

"Little old woman who has a house on the main dock leading from our slip. She knits and watches. Gossip is her trade."

I was familiar with that, being in the info business myself. "Thanks."

"No problem. I'm going to go tie us off." She let go of the wheel and passed by me, hurrying to the bow and jumping off as the boat drifted gently into a little space made just for it.

I followed, leaping off before she had the boat tied up, and gave her a quick wave. "Thanks for the tip."

"No problem. Good luck."

"Thanks."

"Oh, hey." She turned to me. "That angel couldn't keep his eyes off you. And if I were you, I don't think I'd say no."

Neither did I. And that was the problem.

I just nodded and turned, hurrying down the dock that bobbed underfoot. It was still dark out, but dawn would come soon. I hoped Florence was out.

Declan was nowhere to be seen, unfortunately.

About fifty yards later, after I'd passed a half dozen houseboats of varying sizes, I spotted a small woman sitting at the front step of her immaculate houseboat. It was shaped like the sun, perfectly round and bright yellow. Flowers tumbled from window boxes.

Thank fates Florence was an early riser.

The woman's dress was bright purple, and her hands flew

over needles that knitted yarn that looked like liquid silver. I stopped in front of her. "Florence?"

She looked up, eyes bright. "Yes?"

"The ferry captain said that you're the person who sees everything. I wondered if you noticed a demon pass by here a few hours ago."

Her eyes sharpened. "Big one, gray horns, and a green gem in its forehead?"

"That's the one."

She shook her head. "Nope, didn't see him."

"But you just described him!"

She grinned. "Just keeping you on your toes. Yes, I did see him."

"Where did he go?"

She laughed. "As if I'd give away that information for free!"

"Payment?" I could work with that. "What do you want?"

"Let me read your fortune."

"That doesn't sound like payment. Sounds like I'm getting a twofer."

"Do you want your fortune read?"

"Well, no." I really wasn't into that kind of thing. What if it were bad?

"Then it's not a twofer."

"But why do you want to read *my* fortune?"

"I'm bored."

I frowned, not sure that I liked her reasoning. "What else do you want? How about money?"

Mari and I charged so much for our blood sorcery business that I could afford it.

"I already said what I wanted." She kept knitting, her attention wandering from me.

"Fine." I knelt at her side and held out my palm. "Have at it."

"I'm no charlatan." She dropped her knitting needles and

gripped my temples, lifting my face up so I was forced to look into her eyes.

I jerked back, hard, but her grip was too strong. My heart thundered in my ears as her pupils grew wide and consumed her irises. My whole body began to vibrate, as if she were reaching into my soul and shaking me.

Holy fates!

I struggled, trying to break free, but it was impossible.

As quickly as it had started, it ended. The woman removed her hands and sat back, looking younger suddenly.

"Hey!" I stood. "You didn't read my fortune. You stole energy."

It was an uncommon type of magic, and only a few species had it. I couldn't tell what she was, but I was feeling a bit more tired. And she looked a hell of a lot perkier. Magical energy was finite. After using it up, one had to rest. This was the last thing I needed on a demon hunt.

"Tsk-tsk." She shook her head. "I did read your fortune, dear."

"But you also took energy."

"That too." She smiled. "Don't you want to know what I saw?"

"Not really."

"Not the future but the past. You are from Grimrealm."

My skin chilled. "You shouldn't be able to read the past."

That was an extremely rare talent. Even rarer than the energy sucking. What *was* she?

"Well, I can." She gave me a hard look. "You're hunting the demon with a man."

"Not *with* a man."

"That's what you think. But you'll only succeed if you're together."

Yeah, I didn't like the sound of that.

"And you'll want to succeed, dear. Oh yes, you will." Her eyes gleamed with warning.

"What do you mean?"

"Now you're interested?"

"You're really laying it on thick, you know. Of course I'm interested."

"If you don't catch the demon, the secret of your origin will be revealed to the world."

I shrugged, but I doubted I was able to hide the fear that probably shined in my eyes. "So what? There are a lot of people from Grimrealm."

But still, I didn't want it getting out far and wide that *I* was from Grimrealm, not considering that my family was still alive and hunting me and Mari.

"Not that many Dragon Bloods from Grimrealm." Her eyes twinkled, but it was more malevolent than cheerful.

"I'm a Blood Sorceress." The words almost shook as I said them. "I have no idea what you mean by Dragon Blood."

"Whatever you say, dear." The woman shrugged, and I really didn't like her.

Since there was no convincing her away from the truth— she'd seen it herself, after all—I needed to move this conversation along. "The demon? Where did he go? I've given you what you want, so it's your turn."

"He went to visit Marie, the voodoo priestess. I don't know why."

"Where do I find her?"

"Three docks down, four over. Cross the long bridge. She's at the end. But be careful. It's not easy to get to her unless you're invited."

"But not impossible."

"Not impossible."

I nodded, not bothering to thank her. Quick as I could, I

nicked my finger with my sharp thumbnail and let blood rise. Then I lunged, swiping the white blood across her forehead. "Forget of me, I will of thee."

Her eyes glazed over, and the swipe of blood on her forehead faded. Satisfaction suppressed some of the fear that shivered through me. At least she wouldn't remember what she'd seen. Before I'd turned away, she'd already started working on her silver yarn again.

I left her where she was, knitting away, and hurried down the dock. Her directions were easy to follow—three down, four over. I passed by houses that bobbed gently on the bay, all manner of style and color. It was a pretty fantastic place, really.

By the time I'd gone the three over, the atmosphere was distinctly different. There were no more houses, and the dock that stretched out in front of me was long and lonely.

A house sat at the end, a tall three-story structure that leaned slightly left. Green and purple magic swirled in the air around the roof, and it was clear that Marie was up to something. Also, she didn't like neighbors.

I stepped onto the dock that stretched toward her house and jogged over the long expanse. I'd only gone about five meters when it began to undulate beneath my feet. I stumbled, barely managing to catch myself before going into the water.

The dock moved like waves on the ocean, up and down, and it took everything I had to maintain my balance. I *so* did not want to get wet. It was one thing to swim in the ocean. It was another thing to get the wet rat treatment.

Soon, the dock was undulating ten feet in the air.

Ah, crap.

I dropped to my hands and knees and crawled as I clung to the slats. Slowly, I inched over the wobbling bridge.

When the dock flipped over, my heart leapt into my throat. I hung on tightly, my legs dangling over the water as my breath heaved. Beneath me, silver fish rose to the surface, snapping their jaws.

Ah, crap.

This was not piranha territory, but that didn't mean these fish couldn't eat me alive. I began to swing, finally managing to get my legs up onto the dock and pull myself around onto the top side.

It was arched ten feet in the air when it began to flip upright, and I dropped to my hands and knees then scrambled around so I was on top of it as it slammed back into the water. Cold ocean splashed up on me, and the dock began to rise once more.

Holy fates, this had to stop.

I looked around, but saw no one.

Carefully, I slit my finger with my sharp thumbnail. Blood welled, along with my magic. I envisioned breaking the charm on this bridge, forcing it to lie still and normal.

I needed to be *very* careful with this blood magic. It was rare I'd use it three times in a day, but desperate times and all. This was still a slippery slope, creating new magic. As long as I kept it tiny and temporary, I should be okay.

And I had to catch this damned demon.

"Crack and break, my will to make," I murmured. I let my blood drip onto the dock, imagining the spell breaking. Magic snapped in the air, and the dock lay still.

Thank fates.

The fish still snapped their jaws on either side of the dock, but I ignored them and scrambled to my feet. I sprinted toward the house, determined to get this over with.

When the first fish flew out of the water, I didn't see it until it smacked me in the cheek, slicing my flesh. Pain welled.

Freaking fantastic.

More fish.

Another one flew out of the water, leaping toward my head. I ducked, but a third had jumped for me, its sharp fins slicing my arm.

"Ouch!" I winced. My jacket protected against small blades, but these guys were *sharp*.

"Back off or I'll turn you into sushi." I drew my mace from the ether and calmed my mind, making it easier to see and sense the fish as they flew at me.

The spiked ball was a blur as I swung it at them, smacking the fish as they flew through the air. By the time I reached the house at the end of the dock, I was wet and speckled with fish blood, my breath heaving. Fish were impaled on the spikes of the mace.

Ew.

This was *not* going well.

I stopped in front of the door, dunking the mace in the water a few times to dislodge the impaled fish. Once it was clean, I stowed it in the ether. Before my fist could make contact with the door, it swung open.

A beautiful woman leaned against the doorframe, her arms crossed over her chest and her brows raised. Her dark skin glowed with a beautiful light, and her black hair was a riot of curls around her head. The red dress that clung tightly to her figure made her look like she should be walking the catwalk somewhere.

"Marie?" I asked.

"The one and only." She leaned over to look at the dock, which now lay still. "I see you made it all the way here. That's unusual."

"Quite the protection setup you've got going."

"You must be desperate."

"I usually am."

Marie chuckled. "You don't feel dangerous. What do you want?"

"I'm looking for a necromancer demon. *He's* dangerous."

"Of course he is. It's in his name." She looked me up and down. "And you're covered in fish blood."

"Better than fish guts." I gave a weak smile.

She waved a hand in front of her, murmuring something low under her breath. Magic filled the air, the sound of revelers followed by the taste of cognac. My skin tingled, and I looked down.

All the fish blood was gone.

I looked back up at her. "Thanks."

"I had to. Can't let you in otherwise." She turned and waved me inside. "Come on."

I entered a house that was a riot of color. She led me to a room that was laid out similarly to my workshop at home, though it smelled different. The fire crackled, shedding light on the jewel-tone jars that sat on the shelves. I didn't recognize a lot of the ingredients, but then, she was a voodoo priestess and I was a Blood Sorceress.

"Can you tell me where the necromancer demon went?" I asked.

"For a price." She sat in a big chair by the fire and crossed one leg over the other. "What are you?"

"'What can you do for me?' Is that what you mean?"

"Exactly."

"I'm a Blood Sorceress."

Her brows rose, and interest gleamed in her eyes. "Excellent. If you make me a concealment charm—a really strong one—I'll help you."

I frowned. "*You* could probably make one, though, I bet."

"I could. But the person I'm hiding from has the same magic I do. He'd be able to track it and break it." Her dark eyes took on a haunted look, and her skin paled slightly. I decided I hated whoever she was hiding from. Clearly, he'd hurt her and scared the shit out of her. "I need a type of charm he can't detect."

I nodded. Made sense. It'd be tough, though. I chewed my lip, hoping I could pull it off without Mari. We normally worked as a team, and it helped. "Is that why you have the crazy dock that leads to your house?"

"Precisely."

"Okay, I can do a charm if you have the ingredients." I walked toward her shelves, wondering how she made a living if she was hiding out here, away from the rest of town. Maybe her customers had invitations. "Do you have any root of Hesperus?"

"Blue bottle, bottom shelf."

I bent down and grabbed it, then kept searching. "So, who is this guy? Ex-boyfriend?"

I didn't like the idea of her hiding from some ex. That was a shitty way to live, always hunted, ever on the lookout.

I'd know.

"Long ago," she said.

I turned to her. "I could kill him if you like."

I wasn't big into killing, but I'd take out an abuser with a smile on my face. So okay, I was *kind of* into killing. Killing the right sorts. The sorts who had lost their living privileges, as I liked to call it.

She grinned. "I like you."

"I like me, too." I studied her. "So, that's a no on the killing?"

"Maybe if he gets past this concealment charm. But I've got a feeling you want to keep hunting this demon of yours."

"True." I did need to catch this bastard, and a deviation to kill her ex didn't fit into my schedule, no matter how fun it would be. I turned back to the shelves and found a few more ingredients that I needed. There was no time to dawdle.

I set my cache on the table in front of the fire and looked at her. "This will be stronger if you have some of his blood on hand. He really won't be able to find you, then."

She smiled, a bloodthirsty grin, and rose to move quickly to a box that sat on a table on the far side of the room. She withdrew a small dagger and handed it to me. "Will this do?"

I inspected the dark stain on the steel. "Sure will. Too bad you didn't kill him with this, though."

"You're telling me."

I worked quickly, pouring tiny amounts of the liquid ingredients into a small onyx bowl. I turned so that Marie couldn't see and sliced my finger with my thumbnail, used to the pain by now. A few drops of white blood dropped into the bowl, hidden from her view.

"And for the final touch..." I picked up the blade that was coated in the asshole's blood and dipped it into the liquid, then stirred slowly. It began to smoke and sparkle, smelling strongly of lilacs and gasoline.

A weird combo, but it told me it was working.

Once the smoke had turned a dark black, I hovered my left hand over the concoction, feeding my magic into my palm until it glowed a pale white. My magic was in my blood and my soul. Once I combined those two—along with a few select ingredients—things really got hopping.

The smoke rose faster, coalescing beneath my palm until it formed a small silver ball. My vision began to darken as I fed more magic into my palm.

Whew, this is hard without Mari.

Normally, we combined our magical energy. Doing it alone was tough.

Finally, the ball dropped into the wooden bowl. I grinned and set the blade on the table, then picked up the ball and held it out to her. There was a hole through the middle so she could thread a chain through it.

"Keep this on you, and he won't be able to find you." Some charms could be imbued into a person's soul, but I didn't have the time or ingredients to make one of those.

She smiled and took it. "Thank you."

"Now, where can I find the necromancer demon? And what was he looking for?"

"I didn't give him anything, if that's what you're asking."

"But you did tell him how to find what he was looking for."

She shrugged. "He paid."

"Where did he go?"

"Up the mountain to the sacred pool." She walked toward the door and opened it, pointing up at the mountain. "See that path there? You follow it up the road and onto the trail. Then through the tunnel and forest until you get to the gorge at the top. There, you'll find the pool."

I could just barely make out the path that she'd indicated. The sun was about to rise, which would give me more light soon. But it looked like a long way.

"What's in the pool?"

She shrugged. "Stuff."

"Stuff?"

"People say it will give you whatever you want. I don't know though."

But the demon was definitely after something. He'd collected two ingredients from Snakerton, and now he was after something else. This had all the hallmarks of him gathering ingredients for a spell. A big one.

"Thanks." I stepped onto the dock, then turned back to her. "You didn't happen to see a dark-haired guy, did you?"

Her eyes gleamed with interest. "The sexy fallen angel."

Damn. "I suppose you told him how to find the demon too?"

"I did indeed."

"What did he pay with?" No way he had anything as good as my blood sorcery.

She said nothing. Instead, she smiled enigmatically and shut the door in my face.

Annoyance flared. I didn't want to think about what he paid her with, since her smile made it clear enough.

7

I sprinted out of the house, determined to catch that bastard Declan. He had a lead on me, but he wouldn't keep it.

Thankfully, the dock didn't give me any trouble as I ran for the shore. I made my way toward the main collection of houseboats, then cut toward land. It was still quiet out on the water—too early for most—and I made it onto solid ground without seeing a single soul.

The first road leading up the mountains was narrow but paved, lined on either side with beautiful houses made of metal and glass. Magic vibrated from them, indicating supernatural residents, but it was hard to say what species.

I'd nearly reached the more rural forest path when a dark spot in the sky caught my attention. I looked up, breath heaving, and squinted into the darkness. A faint glow had started coming from the horizon, and the rising sun gleamed off of silver wingtips.

Declan.

He was flying up the mountain.

Fast bastard.

But no. I squinted harder. That wasn't just him.

The dark blob in the sky was way too big.

A moment later, with the sun just slightly closer to the horizon, I was able to make out the figure in the sky. It was Declan, wrestling with a huge dark shadow. It looked kind of like a bird, with claws and a beak protruding from a shadowy form. The creature was twice as big as him.

Another shadow bird hurtled from the left, approaching them. Lightning pierced the sky as thunder cracked, hitting the shadowy form. It was a shriek of joy rather than pain, and the creature flew faster.

Declan was too busy fighting the closest monster to notice, his silver sword flashing in the sky. He landed a blow to the creature's chest, and it hissed as black smoke poofed up from the wound.

Black magic.

A guard spell just like the giant squid, no doubt intended to protect the sky route. I grinned as I sprinted faster, determined to make up for lost time. These black magic bird-like creatures were the first good thing to happen today, and I wouldn't waste the advantage.

As Declan fought in the sky, I sprinted up the forest path. I couldn't help but peek upward every few seconds, keeping track of the battle.

Declan was fast and fierce, a vicious fighter who moved with a skill and grace that rivaled even mine. He dodged the claws and beaks while swiftly striking out with his blade.

But there were too many of them. Five of them were driving him toward the ground. I caught sight of his face, illuminated in the light of the rising sun, at the exact moment he looked at me.

He grinned.

The bastard grinned!

Annoyance pushed me faster up the mountain. The path

had become rough dirt, narrow and twisty as it wound upward through the brush.

A half second later, Declan landed about twenty yards in front of me. He had a few bloody wounds—one seeping blood from his upper arm and another at his neck—but it didn't slow him down.

"Nice to see you catching up," he said.

Then he turned and raced up the mountain.

I pushed myself harder, managing not to pant as I shouted, "I think you should keep flying."

"Didn't work like I'd hoped."

I could hear the smile in his voice.

The birds left him alone once he was on the ground. As I'd thought, they were sky guardians, meant to block the quicker, safer path toward the pool at the top.

I sprinter faster, using my unnatural speed, and was nearly to him when I spotted a nice big rock.

I grinned and swooped down to grab it, then hurled it at his back. I could have aimed for the head, but I'd heard a story once about how there was a spot there that would kill you instantly if it was hit.

As much as I wanted to beat him, I didn't want to kill him. He annoyed me, but that wasn't really a killing crime. I might want it to be, but it wasn't.

My rock hurtled through the air and slammed into his back. He went down hard, and I leapt over him, shouting, "See you later!"

Actually, this was pretty fun.

And if I wasn't wrong, I heard him *chuckle*.

What the hell?

I turned back to see him grinning as he stood.

Insane.

The dude was insane.

Maybe as nuts as me.

I picked up the pace, spotting a divergence in the path up ahead. It split into two, each path looking nearly identical as it snaked up the mountain. Prickly bushes separated them. The one on the left looked maybe a little better, so I took that one, racing upward.

I glanced back to see Declan already on his feet. He chose the path on the right.

Shit. Did he know something I didn't?

No time for regret.

I pushed myself harder, sprinting as fast as I could. I was about twice the speed of a normal person, my blood able to deliver the oxygen and energy needed for such speed. Declan was fast, too. Maybe it was his angel powers. I had no idea.

"You're not a normal Blood Sorceress," he shouted. "Even with a spell, you're way too fast."

"I'm not a normal *anything*, buddy." I grinned. "I'm freaking fantastic."

He laughed.

I was still ahead, but barely.

When the first boulder began to roll toward me, I glared at it. Damn it.

I timed it perfectly, leaping over the huge rock as it threatened to crush me.

Next to me, Declan jumped his own boulder.

There was no time to watch him, though, not with more boulders headed my way. They bounced down the mountain, crushing plants and leaving pits in the dirt.

Soon, they were coming so fast I was jumping every ten feet. It was like the hurdles of death, an Olympic sport that I would actually watch. I was sweating and out of breath by the time the boulders stopped coming. I'd nearly been flattened a few times, and Declan was in the lead.

He was approaching a section of the path lined by tall skinny pine trees, and I swore I could feel magic spark in the air. When the first tree limb reached out to smack him, I grinned.

But only for a second.

Because there were pine trees by my path, too.

As soon as I neared them, they struck like whips. I ducked and dived, trying to avoid them in this living video game from hell. It was a race against Declan with obstacles that could behead me.

Pretty fun, actually.

Call me crazy, but I liked a good adventure. And a guy who could keep up with me.

Until one of the tree limbs swiped me across the cheek. Pain flared and blood dripped. I smacked a hand to my cheek and scowled, ducking beneath another as it threatened to take my head off.

Cuts to the face were difficult, because I didn't want anyone knowing about my white blood. My ghost suit was enchanted so any of my blood that landed on it turned red, but I didn't have that luxury with my face.

As I ran, I used the blood on my face to do a bit of healing magic, envisioning the cut closing. The pain faded.

By the time I got past the worst of the trees, Declan and I were neck and neck. Our paths were only about twenty feet apart, and I could see a swipe of blood across his cheek.

The race was too close. Up ahead, I spotted the tunnel that Marie had mentioned. But at this rate, there was no way I would beat him.

My gaze snagged on the small copse of trees ahead of Declan. Most of them were between him and me, and if I could just get them to all blow over at once...

Declan wasn't looking at me, so I acted immediately, slicing my fingertip with my thumbnail. I raised my hand to my mouth so my bleeding fingertip was right in front of my lips, and I blew, envisioning wind.

Just a little bit. One gust. Not permanent magic or anything.

As if a hurricane had burst from my lungs, the wind whipped toward Declan. I jerked my hand down just as the trees bowled over in front of him. He skidded to a stop, staring at the mountain of trees that was piled right in his way.

He wouldn't pause long, that was for sure. I sprinted ahead, almost immediately regretting my actions.

Sure, it'd gotten me the lead and he hadn't seen me.

But I was supposed to be more sparing with this magic.

I shook away the regret and sprinted forward, feeling the burn in my lungs and my muscles. The tunnel was just ahead, a gaping black mouth in the middle of the soaring cliff face.

Right before I reached it, I glanced back at Declan. He was just now leaping off the giant pile of trees, his gaze glued to me.

I hurtled into the darkness of the tunnel, grinning. I'd only gone about ten yards in when magic sparked on the air. It prickled against my skin like bee stings.

"Oh, crap!"

Protective magic. And in a tunnel like this, all kinds of Indiana Jones shit could go down. I was still a good hundred yards from the exit, which glowed in the distance with a faint white light.

When the rumbling started, my skin chilled. I froze, searching the interior of the tunnel. By the time I finally looked up, the ceiling of the tunnel was nearly to my head.

I flung my hands upward, bracing them against the ceiling that was slowly grinding down upon me. The whole top of the tunnel was lowering, and I had a damned strong feeling that it wouldn't quit until I was a pancake in the dirt.

Sweat broke out on my brow as I strained to keep the roof in position. I was crouched down to about seventy-five percent of my normal height, and the thing seemed to have stopped moving. My muscles burned, but I was strong enough to keep it up.

"Having a bit of trouble there?" Declan's voice echoed down the tunnel.

"Crap. You already?"

"You know you're glad to see me."

"Fortunately, I'm facing the other direction." Also fortunate, the tunnel was narrow enough that he couldn't sneak around me while I held up the ceiling.

I tried inching forward while holding up the tunnel roof. It'd be slow going, but maybe I could beat him there, if only by an inch.

I managed it, but the tunnel roof squeaked down another fraction of an inch. Every step forward meant that the roof lowered, and there was no way I'd make it all the way to the end. At best, I could get back out to the entrance, but that would do me no good.

Shit.

"I think you know what this means, right?" Declan asked.

I nearly groaned. "You're going to try to squeeze past me? Because I'm warning you, it's tight in here, and there's no way I'm letting you by."

"I wouldn't object to sharing some tight spaces with you."

I whipped my head around to look at him. From the tiny half smile on his face, he meant that in the way it sounded.

Dirty.

"But now isn't the time," he said. "The only way to get out of this is teamwork."

"Ugh." But since my muscles ached more with every second... "Fine, what's your plan?"

"I'll hold this up while you run through. On the other end, you hold it up for me."

"You trust me not to ditch you." *You shouldn't.* But I was smart enough to keep that bit to myself.

"Yeah."

Right. I wasn't going to look a gift horse in the mouth. "Okay. Let's do it."

"Give me your word, first."

My word was only good when given to Mari. And *maybe* to a few of my friends, who were relatively new additions to my life. But with this guy? Nah.

"Sure, you've got my word." I glanced back to see if he believed me, but it was impossible to read his expression.

He reached up to support the roof, though.

I grinned. "Thanks."

"Thank me by keeping your end of the bargain."

I nodded and lowered my hands, bracing myself. The roof didn't lower. I turned and raced away, crouched low to avoid hitting my head. The light at the end of the tunnel grew nearer, and my heart beat faster.

I was so going to ditch his ass.

I raced out into the sunlight.

"Hey!" Declan shouted.

I stopped dead in my tracks.

Shit.

I turned back to him, debating. For most of my life, breaking my word had been easy. . Mari and I looked out for each other and each other only. But now...

It was harder.

Maybe it was age. Maybe I liked him.

I scowled, stomping back toward the tunnel, pissed as hell with myself but unable to stop. I crouched down and braced my hands against the stone overhead. "All right, come on!"

He gave me one long look—I couldn't see his face from this distance, but damn, I could feel it—then he ran.

Fast.

Like a freaking bullet.

Probably didn't want me to drop the roof on him when he was only halfway across. He'd be squished before he could work his way out.

Just because I was trying to be a decent person didn't mean I had to play *completely* fair. Once he was about ten feet from the exit, I let go of the roof.

He stopped dead, propping his hands on the ceiling to stop if from descending.

"What the hell?" he growled.

"You can get out. It'll be a bit slow, but you'll make it to the end. It's not far."

His scowl deepened, and damned if he didn't look good like that. He started forward, slowly inching along as he held up the ceiling. Every time he shifted his hands along the rock, it dropped another inch. He was nearly to the end though.

I grinned at him. "Eat my dust."

I turned and ran, leaving him to get himself the rest of the way out.

The other side of the tunnel was a massive forest. The trees were huge—like great redwoods or something, towering hundreds of feet in the sky. Morning sunlight filtered through the leaves, falling in dappled rays over the forest floor. It would be beautiful if not for the creepy feeling in the air.

I followed the slope upward, alert for anything out of the ordinary.

At first, there was nothing.

By the time the black cloud darted out from behind a tree and surged toward me, it was almost too late. The thing was about a foot taller than me and twice as wide, a creature surrounded by a haze of black smoke. A lot like the birds that had attacked Declan, but no wings.

The monster was nearly to me when I dived left, skidding on the dead leaves as I barely avoided a swipe of the monster's claws.

Panting, I scrambled upright and turned to face my prey, drawing my mace from the ether as I did so. I hefted the comforting weight as I studied my opponent.

Definitely some kind of smoke demon, with razor-sharp claws of obsidian and fangs that gleamed a bright silver against its hazy form. Another one crept out from behind the trees to my left, and my hair stood on end.

There had to be more of them.

But how many?

No time to wonder. Instead, I swung my mace, getting ready for a big hit, and charged.

The smoke monster came right for me, claws raised. I swung my mace, using so much strength that it tore off the beast's arm. Black blood burst from the wound, and it hissed, slicing out with the other arm. I ducked, narrowly avoiding the silver claws that would have taken a piece out of my cheek.

I whirled to face him again, but he disappeared in a poof of smoke.

Crap.

He wasn't gone for good.

Instinct had me spinning once more, my mace whirling. He'd already appeared behind me. He swiped out with his claws, narrowly missing my neck. I lunged backward, gaining some distance.

He disappeared again.

Behind me.

I spun around, gripping the mace chain with both hands and swinging it in a wide arc. The steel slammed into the demon's middle, and its fiery red eyes widened as it looked at me.

I waved. "Bye-bye."

The creature's entire abdomen was crushed, half the flesh missing and blood spurting. With the life sucked away, the smoke faded, leaving behind a skinny body the color of ash.

I could probably use the blood in some potions, but there was no time. I spun around, searching for the second demon.

Instead, I found three.

They approached as a pack, a leader in the front. Three sets of blazing red eyes stared at me as they raised their claws.

Part of me wished I hadn't trapped Declan back there, but it was such a tiny part it was barely audible. I could get myself out of this.

I charged. Fast as smoke, they disappeared. A moment later, they surrounded me.

I lunged right, swinging my mace. The smoke demon disappeared.

I sensed a figure coming from my right more than I saw it, and I swung my arm toward it, my mace an extension of myself. The steel ball slammed into the smoke monster's head, and it collapsed.

I spun again, finding one right behind me, so close that its claws made contact with my arm. Pain flared, blood dripping, and I stumbled away. I was quick on my feet, though, lunging back toward him as I raised my mace and slammed it against his head.

The third demon was standing close enough that I got lucky. I swung my mace and took him down, using a two-handed swing to cut him right through the middle. It took a hell of a lot of strength, but these guys were skinny enough that it was possible.

"There's more." Declan's voice cut through the sound of my heaving breaths.

I almost groaned at the sound—*I'd lost my lead*—but I spotted the demons he was talking about.

A dozen of them, all surrounding us. They disappeared and reappeared at will, clearly trying to psych us out.

Ha.

As if that would work.

Declan drew his blade from the ether, his gaze serious as he scanned the group.

I edged toward him. "How do you feel about a bit more teamwork?"

"I think it's the only way we'll survive."

8

I moved toward Declan, lining myself up so we stood with our backs to each other. I stashed my mace in the ether and drew a sword. Back to back combat was best with swords, considering that the backswing on my mace could kill Declan.

That would be poor form. Poor form indeed.

The demons flashed in and out of the space around us, getting closer and closer.

I lunged toward one of them, slicing my blade toward its neck. The steel cut through the monster like it was made of butter, and the head toppled to the ground. The body followed.

Behind me, the sound of a demon hissing hallmarked Declan's quick attacks. I backed up, my shoulder touching his lightly so I knew no demons could sneak up on me from behind. Warmth surged through me at the contact.

A demon lunged for me, and I thrust my blade into its middle, then yanked it to the side. The creature hissed and fell backward, but not before landing a swipe to my arm that stung like hell.

Warm blood dripped, turned red by my suit.

I ignored it, lunging for another monster and slicing it

through the middle. A second approached almost immediately after, landing a slice to my thigh. Claws tore through my muscle and agony flared.

Declan and I moved fast, but the monsters were good. They landed almost as many blows as I did. Mine were killing blows, at least. The bodies piled up as we moved in tandem, a deadly dance that was highly effective.

Every inch of my body ached, wounds seeping blood, but finally, the last of the demons lay dead.

"We make a good team," Declan said from behind me. He didn't even sound out of breath.

"Yeah." Panting, I staggered away from him.

I wanted to get a move on, but damn, did I hurt. First things first—I needed to find a place to heal myself. I staggered toward a tree, leaning against the bark and drawing in a deep breath.

Healing was a power that Mari and I had almost given ourselves permanently, but it was too risky. After we'd given ourselves the power of lightning, our signatures had grown. They'd doubled in strength, becoming nearly impossible to hide.

We'd decided we couldn't risk it.

Declan approached, his big body covered in just as many cuts as my own. "Are you all right?"

"Fine." Except for the fact that he was watching me. I didn't want to heal myself in front of him. The last thing I needed was him noticing how I used my magic. He'd eventually figure out that I had a *lot* of unrelated skills that weren't easily explained.

He stepped closer, towering over me.

Boy, he's big.

"You don't look fine." Concern creased his brow. "Let me heal you."

I blinked at him. "Um, how?"

There were all kinds of healing magic, and I definitely didn't want to agree to anything weird.

"Like this." He hovered his hand over my shoulder, magic sparking from him.

Warmth radiated from his palm. Tension prickled over my skin. He wasn't even touching me yet, and my heart was racing.

"You have some kind of healing angel light?" I asked.

"Pretty much."

I only had to think about it for a second before I nodded. This would save me the magic, and there was no way to slip away and heal myself without giving him the lead. "Okay, thanks."

He stood so close that I could almost feel the heat of him, and damn, did he smell good. Like the forest and a cool breeze. My heart started to pound.

"I'm going to touch you now." He spoke in a low tone that brushed over my skin. He probably said it to be polite, but all it did was ratchet up the tension to an unbearable level.

I knew what was coming, and I wanted it.

His hand pressed to my shoulder, and time slowed. Warmth flowed through me as his magic surged into my body. It filled me from within, a glowing light that drove away the pain and knit my wounds back together.

I looked up. His dark gaze was pinned to mine.

A connection formed between us—magic or emotion or desire or *something*. Whatever it was, it was strong.

Unable to help myself, I swayed toward him, my gaze glued to his. As the pain faded from my body, desire took its place. I couldn't help but notice how broad his shoulders were, how full his lips.

I swallowed hard, wanting nothing more than to rise up on my toes and press my lips to his.

Not a terrible idea, right?

Slowly, I rose up on my tiptoes. His hand shifted to cup the back of my neck, warm and strong. My head buzzed with desire, every inch of me prickling with awareness.

He bent his neck, moving toward me.

His lips were nearly to mine when a bird screeched in the distance.

It dragged me out of my haze, and I jumped.

Oh fates, this was a bad idea.

Not only did I have a demon to catch—pronto—kissing the fallen angel was a dumb idea. For one, it'd increase his interest in me. I didn't need that. Nor did I need to grow attached, no matter how much I wanted to lock lips with him.

I pulled back. "Thanks for healing me."

Without meeting his gaze, I slipped to the side and sprinted away, heading through the forest and up the mountain. I ran like the hounds of hell were on my tail, chasing me down.

In a sense, they were. Because this guy lit me on fire.

He had to heal himself, so that would give me a few seconds of lead time. The fact that he'd chosen to heal me before himself —even though he'd been covered in just as many wounds— didn't escape me. Maybe I was a bitch for ditching him, but I had a necromancer demon to kill.

Up head, a massive cliff wall rose high. A narrow gorge cut through it, just like Marie the voodoo priestess had described. I raced for it, glancing back to check on Declan's progress.

A golden light glowed around his body as he healed the cuts that covered him. I turned back and raced into the gorge.

Tall stone walls towered high on either side, and the narrow valley was studded with massive boulders. I darted around them, slowing a bit as I got a hit of dark magic.

I vaulted over a boulder and ducked under a tree root that grew out of the wall to my left. In the distance, a dark blob in the sky caught my eye. I squinted, trying to make out what it was.

It dived low, headed for me.

A moment later, I spotted them.

Bats. Hundreds of bats, out in the daylight.

That alone was weird. Their fangs were even weirder. Long and white and sharp.

They swooped low, aiming right for my head. When they were almost upon me, I ducked. My heart thundered as they whooshed by, their little claws tearing at my hair.

I straightened and looked up, searching for them. They'd spun around in the air and were headed back for me.

Ah, shit.

Quickly, I sliced my finger with my thumbnail and envisioned a flame bursting forth. I turned and blew on my hand. A massive fireball exploded toward the bats, which shrieked and darted away.

Only briefly, though.

They plunged again.

Shit. Could I make enough fire to drive them off?

Maybe not.

Up ahead, a thorny tangle of vines protruded out of the cliff walls on either side. There was about eight feet of space below them—just enough for me to run under.

I sprinted faster, racing for the vines and praying the demon bats didn't like thorns. A few of the little bastards caught up to me, nipping at my shoulders with their sharp fangs.

Pain flared, a taster of what would happen if hundreds of them landed on me.

They'd devour me.

My lungs burned as I pushed myself harder, sprinting beneath the vines. I turned and used the same magic that I had before, blasting a bit of fire at the entrance to the makeshift tunnel. It drove away the few that had followed me in.

The bats shrieked their rage, flying away.

I sprinted through the tunnel, looking up through the thorny vines. The bats flew overhead, trying to find a way to get to me, but they couldn't. The vines were too thick, and the bats were too stupid to fly low to the ground and enter the tunnel the same way I had. Or my fire had scared them off.

Either way, they disappeared within seconds, no doubt off to find easier prey. I hurried through the tunnel, finally reaching the end of the vines. The cliff walls still towered high on either side of me, but my thorny ceiling was gone.

I looked up, heart thundering, and searched the sky for bats.

None.

Thank fates.

I kept up my pace, darting around boulders and looking up to search for bats.

Magic prickled on my skin as I navigated between the boulders. It grew stronger and stronger, making my stomach turn.

Something was coming.

Not just Declan, who had to be gaining on me from behind.

I reached out with my magic, trying to get a feel for what was headed toward me. I couldn't tell exactly, but there was darkness in the air here. A protective charm that would hurt when it finally went off.

When the ground dropped out from beneath me, a scream tore from my throat. I plummeted, my stomach hurtling upward, and reached for something. Anything.

Except there were no tree roots to grab onto, and no ledges. Just smooth wall as I fell into a huge pit in the ground.

Shit!

I needed to create some magic. Something to get me out of this. Growing wings was too complicated for a little spell like the ones I normally used to create wind or make suggestions to people.

Think, think. I can do this.

I could conjure a grappling hook.

Something appeared above me, shooting downward. A massive dark figure with wings. In half a second, I was swept up into strong arms. I stopped falling immediately, my stomach plunging back into place so hard that I nearly puked. My head spun.

Declan.

I clung to his broad shoulders. *Oh, thank fates.*

Concern darkened his eyes, and his massive wings moved close to his body as we rose slowly through the tunnel.

"Mind if I save you this time?" he asked.

"Yeah, it's fine." I probably would have thought of something before I'd smashed to the ground, but I was no moron. This was much easier and safer. I'd actually *wanted* to fall into the ocean. But here? Nah, I was happy with getting a lift. "Thanks."

The edge of his mouth quirked up in a smile. "Anytime."

A tiny flare of heat triggered in my middle, and I suddenly realized how good he felt. All coiled muscle and strength. How much warmth his body channeled into mine. I resisted clinging harder to him as we approached the mouth of the hole I'd fallen into.

I had some restraint, after all. Though if I wasn't going to go for this indulgence, I kind of wanted some Cheetos. Maybe a chocolate bar.

"You don't strike me as the type to walk into a hole," he said.

"An illusion." I shuddered at the memory of the ground dropping out from beneath my feet. "I could feel that there was magic in the air but couldn't figure out what kind of spell it was from. By the time I'd put my foot down, I was already falling."

"Well, you broke the illusion, at least. Because the hole is obvious now."

"Thank fates. I don't want to step into another."

Declan flew out of the hole and into the gorge. I could no

longer feel the dark magic prickling on the air, and he was right. The hole in the ground yawned beneath us, totally visible. When I'd fallen in, the spell must have triggered and snapped. Someone would have to cast it again or it would rebuild itself, but that was a more difficult type of magic.

I didn't want to be around to find out which it was.

I pointed to the far end of the hole on the side where I was heading. "You can drop me there."

"You don't want a ride?" He grinned, his smile devastatingly sexy. "Because I certainly don't mind holding you."

I pointed to the gorge ahead of us. Roots had grown out of the two walls on either side, and they formed a barrier through the middle of the gorge. Just like the one that had protected me from the bats. The only way to get any farther was on foot.

"Not possible," I said.

He looked up, brows rising. "Seems I was distracted."

He looked at me.

The implication was obvious.

"You can just put me down now, thanks." I was getting entirely too warm and antsy in his arms. Like I wanted to kiss him.

And kissing him was almost the exact opposite of chasing down the necromancer demon.

Declan set me on the ground, and I didn't waste any time.

"Thanks." I sprinted away from him, through the gorge. Without the dark magic crackling in the air, I could be fairly confident that another hole wasn't going to open up under my feet.

Though I didn't look back to see Declan behind me, I could feel him. He was right on my tail. Man, he was fast. Anyone who could keep up with me had to have a bit of supernatural speed.

Up ahead, the gorge ended, opening up into a grove of some

kind. I could make out trees and a blue glow. More dark magic prickled on the air, but this was different. This was no spell.

It was the signature of a demon. It smelled of dead bodies and rot and decay.

Necromancer demon.

I picked up the pace, sprinting as fast as I could. No matter what, I'd beat Declan to this damned demon. If the fallen angel had a transport charm on him, he could disappear with my prey in the blink of an eye.

Not on my watch.

I conjured a dagger from the ether, ready to hurl it at the demon as soon as I saw him.

A moment later, I raced into the clearing. It was an enormous pit in the ground, at least the size of a football field. Cliffs rose tall on all sides, putting us in an arena filled with tall pine trees and pillars of rock.

But it was the glowing blue pool in the middle of the space that caught my eye. Magic pulsed from it lightly. The scent of the necromancer demon was fading, as if he were no longer nearby. It cleared the air so I could smell the pool, which had the faint, fresh scent of water overlaid with a floral aroma.

Quickly, I scanned the rest of the space, searching for the demon. I could just barely smell him, though I couldn't see him. He had to be somewhere in this weird arena grove. I just had to find him.

A pillar of rock to my right caught my eye. It hung out over the pool and was a perfect vantage point. I raced toward it and scrambled up the rock until I reached the top, about twenty feet in the air.

To my left, Declan appeared at the exit of the gorge. He scanned the space quickly, and I left him to it, turning my gaze toward the pool below me.

It glittered an inviting blue, and within, a shadow swam. A big shadow. A vaguely demon-shaped shadow.

He's in the damned pool.

Hell yeah.

Probably retrieving something, just as Marie had said.

I crouched low, keeping my dagger at the ready. I'd just wait and nail him as soon as he surfaced. The element of surprise would be on my side.

Though the water was clear, it rippled and pulsed with blue light, making it hard to see exactly what the demon was doing. I glanced over toward Declan, my jaw dropping.

He'd shucked off his shirt and was removing his boots.

Holy fates, he was ripped.

I blinked stupidly, staring at him, then scowled.

The bastard was going to ruin my surprise. He'd spotted the demon, too, and was going to go after him.

Damn it.

"Why don't you come in?" Declan shouted up at me. "Water looks good."

Argh. I didn't bother responding.

If he was going in the water, that meant I was going in the water. And I wasn't about to waste time. I didn't even bother shucking off my boots—I was a strong enough swimmer that they wouldn't bother me.

I gripped my blade tightly and sucked in a deep breath, then dove into the pool. The cold water closed around me as I plunged deep. Immediately, I opened my eyes. Bright blue assailed me, and my vision was slightly distorted due to the pressure of the water.

I searched for the demon, kicking around in a circle.

There.

He was right behind me, swimming up from the bottom. His

grey form was even bigger than I'd anticipated, like some massive horned shark.

Looks like I'm going fishing.

I kicked hard toward him, swimming as fast as I could through tall spires of brilliant green seaweed and past sparkling fish. The magic in the water pulsed around me.

Nearly to him.

Up close, I spotted the big bag in his right hand. It was a rough leather bag closed up with a drawstring, and I'd bet my year's salary from the Apothecary's Jungle that it was full of the ingredients for whatever evil necromancer shit he had planned. In his other hand, he gripped a black glass dagger.

An obsidian athame.

The ancient knives were a relatively rare tool used in magic —he must have recovered it from the bottom of this pool and not yet stuffed it in his bag.

The demon's head jerked as he spotted me swimming toward him. I gripped my blade tight and kicked hard, reaching him a second later.

I swung my dagger, the water pulling on my arm so my motions were slow and sluggish. The steel pierced the demon's arm, and he shouted but didn't drop the dagger. Bubbles poured from his mouth, and I could just barely hear the roar through the water.

He swung his other arm toward me. It was the hand that gripped the bag, and he slammed the leather into me so hard that I tumbled backward through the water, my head aching.

Disorientation gripped me, and I kicked, trying to figure out which way was up. Which way led back toward the demon. He'd hit me so hard that it was obvious there wasn't anything breakable in the bag. Rocks, more like.

My lungs were starting to burn, but I still had a few seconds left in me. Frantic, I searched for the demon.

Instead, I spotted Declan. Then my prey.

The fallen angel was swimming fast, and he'd nearly reached our target. The demon was alert now. The dagger was no longer in his hand, so he must have shoved it in his bag. And he was only about fifteen feet from the surface. But he'd spotted Declan coming for him. He kicked, turning in the water to face the fallen angel. Declan didn't have a weapon on him.

Nope. The dumb bounty hunter was trying to take him alive. I'd felt the strength in those muscles. He'd have a damn good shot.

The necromancer demon shot toward Declan, and I felt the first pang of fear.

That was weird.

The demon should be running.

Declan neared the demon and grabbed for him. The bastard struck out with his hand and smacked Declan in the head.

Dumb demon. A punch underwater, where the viscous liquid slowed your strike, wouldn't hurt a supernatural. Especially not a fallen angel.

Except, it did.

As soon as the demon's fist made contact with Declan's head, a dark light pulsed from his hand. It reverberated through the water, and I got the strongest sense of despair. It washed over me, a feeling that tore at my mind and heart.

Death.

Declan tumbled backward, his body limp.

9

Holy fates!

The demon had some kind of insane death magic. Necromancer demons were dangerous—they were strong, excellent fighters who could raise the dead. But I'd *never* heard of one wielding some kind of sonic boom death power with their fist.

But this one did.

I could still feel the magic reverberating through my chest, a weird kind of power that was a combo of existential despair and cold, hard physical force. My chest ached more than ever.

Damn, I was lucky he'd only hit me with his bag.

As the demon kicked away, Declan floated limply in the water. His body was still fifteen feet from the surface, and there was no guarantee he'd regain consciousness in time to swim there.

If he ever did.

Cold fear shot through me. *He could already be dead.*

Only luck had saved me. I'd swum for the demon just like Declan had, with no idea of the insane power he held in his fist.

Damn it. The angel had saved me back in the gorge.

I gave the demon one last longing look, and swam toward

Declan. My muscles and lungs burned desperately as I approached. I was running out of time down here.

I grabbed Declan by the arm and swam toward the surface. My head broke through toward the air, and I sucked in a deep breath, yanking Declan up with me. I gave him a hard shake, and he gasped, opening his eyes.

"You good?" I demanded.

"Yeah." His gaze was confused and his face pale, but he was still kicking.

"Favor repaid." I let go of him and spun away, racing toward the demon who was swimming across the surface of the lake toward the shore.

He was only twenty yards away from me. I could totally catch him.

And kill him from afar. After what had happened to Declan, no way I was going to get too close to that beast. The demon reached the shore and climbed out onto the rocks. I swam faster, pushing myself to the limit.

I reached the pebbled beach only seconds after him, scrambling out onto the rocks as he ran away, digging into his pocket. He was going for a transport charm, no doubt.

I had only seconds.

I leapt to my feet and hurled my dagger, aiming straight for his back. The silver dagger glinted in the light as it hurtled toward him. Right as it neared the demon, he stumbled on a rock. His body dipped low, and the dagger plunged into his shoulder instead of his back.

Damn it.

The demon whirled, rage twisting his face. His skin was a pale, creased gray, and his horns rose high above his head. He had an enormous green gem in his forehead, and his eyes burned like fire. Fangs hung over his lips, which pulled back in a snarl.

Damn, this guy was ugly.

And scary.

He could cause a hell of a lot of problems all on his own, even without raising the dead.

He stepped toward me, the kind of threatening movement that shouted, *It's time to throw down, bitch.*

Fortunately for him, that was my idea of a good time. If I'd gone to a normal school—or any school—I'd have been voted *Most Likely to Throw Down.*

I withdrew another dagger from the ether and hurled it right toward his chest. The key to winning in combat was to aim for big targets. Weaken them, then go for the kill.

He reached up to stop the blade, but he was too slow. It slammed into a spot right over his heart.

Then bounced off. Two tiny objects flew off the demon's chest. A broken medallion?

It was impossible to see from here. But something had stopped my blade.

The demon laughed, a rusty sound that made the hair on the back of my neck stand up. Rage lit in my chest.

"Oh, you bastard," I muttered. I drew my mace from the ether and charged, my strides eating up the ground.

I neared the demon and swung for the throat, glad that my mace chain was long. My hits were weaker when the chain was long, but I wanted to play it safe. The beast dodged backward just in time, avoiding my blow. I swung again, and the mace's spikes grazed his arm.

Damn, he's fast.

Way too fast for a hulking, eight-foot tall demon. He towered over me. The scent of death that wafted off him clogged my lungs and made my eyes water.

His blade-like nose twitched as he sniffed the air, and his eyes widened as they met mine.

"Dragon blood?" he rumbled.

Ice chilled my veins. He'd *smelled* my true species?

Shit.

I swung my mace, powering up for a big blow, and the demon raised a massive hand. Huge claws sprouted from his fingertips, each at least eight inches long.

"Freaking Wolverine?" *Just my luck.* I swung the mace.

He was fast, reaching out to swipe at my steel chain with his claws. They collided with a clang of metal against metal, and the chain severed. The spiked ball flew into the forest.

Shit!

I dodged backward, tripping over something and slamming into a rock. Pain flared.

Fates, I wished I could activate my ghost suit. But Declan would definitely think something was up if I suddenly disappeared.

Groggily, I raised my head. Through bleary eyes, I saw the demon thrust his free hand into his pocket. He yanked his hand out of his pocket, clutching something.

The transport charm.

I scrambled to my feet, clumsy from disorientation.

Declan sprinted past me, a massive sword in his hand.

Hell yeah! He was going to kill him.

Finally.

Declan swung his blade for the demon's closest arm—the one that gripped the bag full of loot. He was fast and deadly strong. In one swoop, he amputated the limb. It dropped to the ground, the potion bag slamming on the rock. Black blood spurted.

The demon roared, rage in his eyes.

As Declan drew his sword back, clearly going for the other limb, the demon threw the transport charm to the ground. A poof of silver dust rose in front of him. He moved unnaturally fast, lunging toward his dropped bag and grabbing it up, then jumping into the silvery cloud.

The ether sucked him away.

"Damn it!" I stumbled backward, tripping over a root. I landed on my butt, gasping.

Pain radiated through my back. When the demon had chucked me backward, I must have smashed hard into the rock behind me and was just now starting to feel a few broken ribs.

Damned demon. Damned Declan.

"You went for the arm," I accused.

"He can't give me a death punch without any arms." Declan scowled and stashed his sword in the ether. "But he was faster than I expected."

Declan was right. At the end there, the demon had moved quicker than I'd ever seen a demon move. Between his death punch and his speed, he was a species of necromancer demon that I'd never encountered before.

Something special, and deadly.

"I can't believe you tried to take him alive," I muttered.

"It's my job."

Disgusted, I shook my head, which suddenly felt like it weighed a million pounds. I bent my neck, and suddenly I was exhausted. With my face tilted toward the ground, my gaze landed on a bronze medallion. *Half* of a bronze medallion.

I frowned.

The demon's necklace. That medallion had stopped my dagger, which had split it in half. I reached out, hovering my hand over the small piece of metal. No way I was touching anything of the demon's without testing it first.

Dark magic radiated from it, but it was minimal. Nothing like what he'd thrown at Declan. There was definitely a distinct magical signature, though. I gripped the half medallion and clutched it tight.

I could use this to track the bastard.

Trying to be sneaky, I slipped the charm into my pocket and stood, my body aching. Maybe I should look for the other half?

I ran my gaze over the ground around me, but didn't see anything. I glanced up at Declan to see if he'd noticed, but he was staring over my head, his eyes widening.

"Ah, crap."

That was never good. I turned and looked up, spotting a horde of bats swooping toward us. This crowd made the last one look tiny. There had to be thousands, and each one had glinting white fangs. They were hunting for blood.

My blood.

My heart rate spiked.

There was no handy cover like there had been in the gorge. This time, the bats would have direct access.

Time to go.

As the bats neared, I dug into my pocket and grabbed a transport charm just like the demon had done.

"Aerdeca!" Declan shouted, clearly getting an idea for what I was about to do.

Ditch him.

Hell yeah, I was ditching him. No way I was sharing my clue —the medallion—with the guy who'd just lost our prey.

I turned to him. "You got a transport charm?"

"Yeah."

"See you later, then." He could get out of here himself, and I'd let him.

The bats were right overhead when I chucked the transport charm to the ground. A cloud of gray dust poofed up, and I stepped into it, letting the ether suck me away. The last thing I saw was Declan, scowling at me.

～

I appeared in the foyer of my townhouse a second later. As soon as the safety of home enveloped me, exhaustion crashed over me. The halls were dark, and no light filtered in through the windows.

Night had arrived.

"Mari?" I shouted.

"Here!" She sounded just as tired as I felt. A second later, she stumbled into the hall, coming from the direction of her apartment. She still wore her black fight wear, and her hair was a complete rat's nest. Her black eye makeup was streaked around her eyes, with an addition of soot on her cheeks and forehead.

"Looks like you had fun," I said.

"You too." She pointed to my head. "You've got a little seaweed there."

I pulled it out of my hair and winced at the feeling in my back. Definitely some cracked ribs. "You have any luck?"

"Almost. Portal closed—violently—before I could get in."

"That's what's up with the new look?" I gestured to my face and hair, indicating the soot and rat's nest.

"No, I was just trying this out for something new," she deadpanned.

"Well, I like it." I groaned, leaning against the stair railing. "I need a healing potion, then some food, then a nap. But I also need to ask you about this thing I found."

"I hope it's a clue."

"I think it is."

"I'll get you that potion, and we can meet at your place."

"Chinese work for you?"

"Heck yeah."

I stumbled toward my apartment, every inch of me aching. The last little bit of that adventure had really kicked my ass. Home sweet home welcomed me as I stepped into the pristine white space. The truth was that I'd paid a pretty penny for a tidying spell to keep the place so nice, and it was worth every penny.

I went to the little bell that sat on the counter and rang it twice, indicating two portions.

But one of the best investments I'd ever made was installing a tiny portal that led right to a Chinese restaurant down the street. It was enchanted so only food could be passed through, and anyone who tried otherwise would get an explosion to the face. A little added security measure.

I had an account with the Jade Lotus, and whenever I rang the bell, they passed through some food and charged my credit card.

Modern magic was a thing of beauty.

Especially when it meant I could get some deep-fried General Tso's chicken without ever picking up the phone. I had a real thing for junk food that I knew was bad.

The thing was, I just didn't care.

As I waited for Mari and the food, I grabbed a half full bottle of wine. As much as I might like a martini right now, I was once again too exhausted to make one.

I sloshed the wine into two glasses—just a bit, since I'd be off hunting this demon again after a quick recovery nap—and collapsed in the chair.

Mari appeared a moment later, raising a tiny vial in her hand. "Got it."

"You're a lifesaver." I groaned as I reached for the potion, then swilled it back.

Warmth filled me as the meds raced through my body, magically healing my bones and limbs. Relaxation made me sag in the chair as memories of Declan filled my mind. When he'd healed me, it'd felt amazing.

"What's that look for?" Mari asked.

"Uh, nothing." I sipped the wine, then pushed her glass toward her. "Drink your wine. You look like you need it."

"Do I ever." She sipped, then studied me with keen eyes. "You're thinking about the hot angel. How'd that go?"

"The dick lost our mark."

"Dick? That's a little Freudian, isn't it?"

"Jerk. He's a jerk."

"Too late." She grinned at me. "And as much as I want to grill you about him, I guess it'll have to wait. Tell me about the demon."

I nodded and dug into my pocket, then pulled out the half medallion. I pushed it across the table toward her. "The demon got away, but not before this fell off him."

Mari grabbed it and raised it to her face, studying it. She frowned, her brow creased. "This looks familiar."

"It does?" I held my hand out, wiggling my fingers in a grabby motion.

She handed it over, and I squinted at it. I hadn't given it a good look before—I'd been too busy trying to hide it from Declan. But now that she'd said it...

The medallion had half a symbol that did look familiar, but...

"I can't place it." I looked up at Mari. "Can you?"

"No. But something lit up inside me when I saw it."

"Maybe it's from Grimrealm." I shivered at the idea.

Mari's gaze flicked toward the oven, as if she didn't even want to talk about it.

I handed the medallion back to her. "Can you track it?"

Mari had more permanent magic than I did. The dangerous, dragon blood kind of magic that increased our signatures and made us easier to detect and find. It was the main reason she was so committed to her disguise.

She was the oldest, and when we'd been kids and our family had been experimenting with our powers—or forcing us to experiment—she'd gotten the brunt of it. As a result, she had more skills.

One of those skills was tracking. We told the world that she had a bit of Seeker power, and she did. It was just *how* she got it that we didn't tell.

Mari took the charm and held it to her chest. Her eyes drifted shut and her magic swelled on the air, bringing with it the burn of whiskey. A moment later, her eyes popped open. "There's something missing."

"Missing?"

"Yes. It's like there's half a magical signature attached to this medallion. I could track it if I had the other half."

Damn it. I should have looked for the other half. Except for the bats. I really hadn't been in any shape to deal with the bats. "We've got other options."

Mari nodded. "We can try to make a tracking charm."

We made them occasionally, though they were difficult and expensive.

The bell on the counter rang, and two white cartons appeared through the portal.

I jumped up. "I'll just bring this with us." I leaned over and grabbed the bag of Cheetos near the fridge. "And these."

"Nothing like a little blood sorcery and dinner." Mari grinned. Most people would find it gross, but we were well used to it by now. "But you eat like a teenage boy."

"Bring wine. Teenage boys don't drink wine." I raised my brows. "So, yeah. I'm a grown-ass woman."

Mari grinned and grabbed the glasses, and I followed behind her with the food. As much as I was dying for a nap, we didn't have time to dawdle on this demon hunt.

We reached the workshop, and I flicked on the light with my elbow, then set the food on the table. Quickly, I went to the hearth and took a pinch of the magical dust that sat in a bowl on the mantel. I tossed it into the hearth, and the flames burst to life.

Mari grabbed a carton of lo mein and ate while she moved from shelf to shelf, collecting ingredients for the charm. It should have been impossible to do both at the same time, but she was a pro. "I think we should do the determination spell to start."

"I agree." There were a number of ways to use an object to find someone, but first, we'd have to determine if the medallion had what it took to work in a charm. It needed some of the demon's magic, or it had to be very important to him, for it to work for our purposes. Some of the charms destroyed the object, and I didn't want to do that if the spell wouldn't work.

I joined Mari, devouring bites of chicken in between collecting ingredients.

Finally, we had it all laid out on the table, and I'd scarfed down my entire container of chicken. The Cheetos would have to wait. I didn't want any orange dust getting into the potion we were about to make.

Mari and I had been doing blood sorcery for so long that working together was second nature. We were slow from exhaustion, but our movements were flawless as we uncorked vials and poured them into the bowl. I could pretty much sense what she would do next, so it was easy to work as a team.

We make a good team.

Declan's words echoed in my ears. I shook my head, driving off the thought of the sexy angel, and focused on my work. Finally, the liquid in the stone bowl swirled with a metallic green light. I looked at Mari and picked up the medallion.

"Ready?"

She nodded.

I put the medallion in the liquid, careful not to touch it or let it splash. Together, Mari and I held our hands over the potion, nicking our thumbs with our nails. Two droplets of blood fell into the potion—one white and one black—and a gray steam sizzled upward.

"Damn." My shoulders sagged.

"The medallion won't do it." Mari frowned.

It wasn't important enough to the demon, nor imbued with enough of his magic, to help us make a tracking charm.

"We have to go ask the FireSouls." They were the only ones who could possibly help me now. Otherwise, I'd have to head all the way back to that pool and see if I could find the second half of the medallion.

"If anyone can do it, they can," Mari said.

The FireSouls could find almost anything. They each shared a soul with a dragon, and if there was one thing that dragons liked, it was treasure. As a result, the FireSouls could find almost anything of value, since anything could become treasure if you wanted it badly enough.

And damn, did I want to find this demon.

If only my dragon blood could give me the FireSoul's ability to find things.

Mari pulled her phone out of her pocket. "I'll just text them. See if any are around."

The three FireSouls—Nix, Cass, and Del—all lived on Factory Row on the other side of town. I grabbed the bag of Cheetos and dug in, chowing down as we waited.

My shoulders relaxed as the magic of neon orange cheese dust went to work. I wasn't proud of my addiction, but there was no way I was giving it up. Cheetos also went surprisingly well with wine and martinis, which was a fun fact I thanked fates for.

A moment later, Mari's phoned dinged. She read it, then looked up. "Out of town, but they'll be back early tomorrow."

I nodded. "It's fine."

The demon had to deal with his amputated arm, after all, so it gave me a bit of time to sleep, which I desperately needed. It was dangerous to hunt deadly creatures while being so exhausted that you could barely walk, much less fight.

"First thing tomorrow, we'll find the FireSouls," Mari said.

"And that damned demon."

And probably Declan.

10

I n the morning, Mari and I dressed in our fight wear. With what was on the horizon, we'd need it. However, right before we left the house, we both applied our usual going-out glamours.

In truth, she really was wearing the plunging black dress and bouffant about fifty percent of the time. Half our business was staying in and doing blood sorcery, or gathering useful info to sell. Frankly, with the way my body was feeling after all the fighting—like I'd been run over by a dump truck—I wouldn't hate a day at home wearing silk and doing a bit of sorcery.

Like a snow day from demon killing.

It was not in the cards, however.

As I stepped out of the foyer, I stopped in front of the mirror, smoothed my pale hair back, and schooled my features into an icy expression. It worked well with the sleek white outfit I wore. Or, at least, the sleek outfit that it *looked* like I wore. My ghost suit would keep me warm—and if necessary, invisible.

"Come on," Mari said from the stoop. "You look suitably icy. Let's go."

I grinned at her. "As if you didn't already do this."

"Fine, I did."

I gave myself one last look. Aerdeca stared back at me, cold and powerful. No one from my old life would ever make the connection.

I joined her on the step. Sometimes, our charade became tiring. Not that I minded the look or the persona or the clothes —they *were* me. It was *remembering* to make sure I looked right that was annoying.

But it brought with it the freedom of knowing our family would never find us, so it was worth it. Our new look combined with our concealment charm hid us perfectly.

Mari led the way, cutting down the alley to the right of the house. I couldn't help but wonder what Declan was doing right now. Was he farther along on the hunt than I was?

Better not be.

I shoved the thought away and followed Mari to her car, a classic Mustang with a custom paint job—black sparkles, of course. Mari slid behind the wheel and I joined her in the car. She turned the car on. The engine roared, far louder than a normal car, and I smiled at her.

"What?" She shrugged. "I like it."

"It suits you."

She took off for Factory Row, where the FireSouls lived.

I pulled the half medallion out of my pocket and studied it, trying to figure out why the image on the front looked familiar. I couldn't place it though.

As the sun rose higher in the sky, Mari drove down the old street in the Historic District, past buildings that looked a lot like they were from Darklane, except for the fact that they weren't covered in black grime. Next, we went through the business district, between the towering glass buildings that speared toward the sky, then toward Factory Row. The neighborhood where the FireSouls lived was really quite cool. It was mostly a collection of old, nineteenth century factory buildings that had been converted into apartments and shops about a decade ago.

"I cannot *wait* for a coffee," Mari said.

I grinned. We'd be meeting the FireSouls at Potions & Pastilles, a coffee shop and bar run by our friends Connor and Claire.

Mari pulled the car over and parked across the street from the old four-story factory building. Huge glass windows glittered, and the old brick looked charming rather than rundown.

I climbed out, my gaze on the warm interior of Potions & Pastilles. The place was filled with wood furniture and colorful paintings. Mason jar lamps hung from the ceiling, shedding a golden light on the nearly empty space. It was all very hipster Oregon, and though it wasn't my usual style, I'd grown to love it.

The smell of pastries and coffee welcomed me as I stepped in.

Connor looked up, his dark hair flopping against his forehead as he grinned.

"Aerdeca. Mordaca. Long time, no see." His English accent was still pretty thick despite the fact that he'd lived in the States for years. His band T-shirt—today, it was Jim Croce—was covered in smatterings of white flour. Connor was a hearth witch with some badass potion-making powers.

"Hey, Connor." I grinned at him. "Cass come by, yet?"

"Not yet. What can I get you?"

"Espresso, please, two shots." I approached the counter, eying the pastries within.

Mari followed behind me. "A vanilla latte for me, please."

"Coming right up." He got to work at the gleaming silver espresso machine.

The door behind the counter swung open, and Claire strode out. Connor's sister was as tall as he was, with sleek brown hair and a big grin. While she had a bit of hearth witch ability—

nothing like Connor—she was also a fire mage and a mercenary for the Order of the Magica.

Against all odds, she'd become one of my favorite people over the years. Mari and I weren't used to having friends—not after years of charades and hiding—but these two were weaseling their way in.

"Aerdeca, Mordaca! Good to see you." Claire grinned.

They didn't know our real names, however.

Claire went right to the pastry case and grabbed three huge cinnamon buns.

"You know the way to my heart, that's for sure," I said.

She looked at me, frowning. "Strange to see you here this early. What's wrong?"

"Nothing much. Just meeting Cass."

Claire's brows rose, and she clearly knew I was full of shit. Connor put our coffee cups on the counter and grinned. "On the house."

"Thanks."

"Connor, we're sitting. Call me if you need help." She nodded her head toward a table in the far corner. "Come on. Let's go."

I saluted and followed her to the table, Mari at my side.

Claire set the three cinnamon buns down and sat. We joined her, and she leaned on her elbows and gave us a hard stare. "Something is wrong."

"We're fine." Mari bit into the cinnamon bun, a tried-and-true trick to deflect the need to talk by filling your mouth.

"You're not fine," Claire whispered, glaring.

Claire was the only one who knew that we weren't just Blood Sorceresses. She didn't know we were Dragon Bloods, but she did know we lived a bit of a lie and hunted demons for more than just their blood. We hadn't intended to tell her as much as we had, but her mercenary work brought her to

Grimrealm occasionally and she was a good demon-hunting ally.

We could also trust Connor and our friends the FireSouls—Cass, Del, and Nix.

Logically, I *knew* that. They were good people with secrets of their own. They'd understand and have our backs.

But Mari and I didn't care. We'd kept our secrets so long that we wanted to keep them even longer. Maybe it prevented us from developing real and lasting friendships. Maybe we were fucked up and needed therapy.

Whatever. Better safe than sorry.

"Well, what's going on?" Claire demanded.

"Might as well tell her," Mari said.

I nodded. Quickly, I filled her in about the demon with the possible connection to Grimrealm. My stomach grumbled, so I sipped my espresso gratefully, then chomped into the cinnamon bun. Sugar and butter exploded on my tongue.

"Damn, Connor is good at this," I muttered.

"Don't change the subject." Claire leaned forward. "So, this demon may go back to Grimrealm. Or there's info there. Is that it?"

"That's what we think." I took another bite of the cinnamon bun.

"I can go for you if you need," she said.

"No, you can't." Mari shook her head hard. "Last time you ran a job there, you pissed off a mob boss. If you get caught, you're dead."

"If *you* get caught there, you're dead," she said. "Or enslaved, at least."

"That's our problem," I said. "Just like this is." I reached for her hand and squeezed. "But thank you. You're a good friend."

She shrugged.

The bell over the door rang, and I turned to see Cass hurry

in, her red hair still wet from the shower. She wore her usual uniform of a brown leather jacket and jeans.

She shot a grin at us. "Sorry I'm late!"

I turned to her and crossed my legs, smiling. "Thanks for coming."

"Of course." She sat, giving Connor a nod, no doubt to confirm her usual order. Cass lived only a few doors down, so she was in here all the time. She looked me up and down. "I don't know how you look so put together all the time."

"Just natural, I guess." I gave her a small smile.

Connor brought Cass a steaming cup and a scone, then retreated back toward the counter. The morning rush would come soon, and he'd probably want to be ready.

"So, what are you looking for?" Cass asked.

"How do you know we're looking for anything?" Mari asked.

"Come on, Mordaca." She tilted her head down and gave my sister a knowing look. "You guys never hang out just to hang out, even though we invite you all the time. Hence, this is about business."

I sighed, feeling a bit guilty. Part of me *did* want to hang out more. A bigger part of me didn't know how, and it was just easier to hang with Mari.

"Okay, you're right," I said. "It is business. No matter what we've tried, we can't make a tracking charm out of this." I dug into my pocket and handed her the half medallion.

She took it and frowned at it, her brow creasing. "What is this?"

"Don't know. A demon was wearing it, and I want to find him."

"For his blood," Cass said.

It wasn't a question. She'd bought our story about hunting demons for their blood for our shop. Why wouldn't she? She was our friend and she trusted us.

A bit of guilt stabbed me, but it was easy to shove away.

"Exactly," Mari said.

"Well, I can try." Cass closed her eyes, her magic swelling on the air. It smelled like a fresh forest breeze and felt like a strong wind. Her dragon sense—that ability to find things of value—often relied upon having a bit of information or an object to ignite it. Something that could give her a little clue to go on—like a magical bloodhound.

Cass kept her eyes closed for longer than I was used to, and I shot Mari a look. She frowned. So did Claire.

Damn, this couldn't be good.

Cass's green eyes popped open. "I'm sorry. I need the whole thing. I'm only getting half images, and it's not enough to decipher."

Damn it. I should have stuck around and looked for the other half.

Except for the bats. They'd have torn me apart.

"Then I need to go get the other half." I cursed. That would take time. I hadn't seen where that thing had flown when my dagger had blasted it apart.

This would definitely put Declan in the lead.

The bell over the door jangled again, and the back of my neck prickled. A sense of awareness rushed over me. My heart began to pound. I turned.

As if he'd heard me thinking of him, Declan stood in the doorway. Tall and broad, with his dark hair sweeping back from his face and his inscrutable gaze pinned to me, he looked like the fallen angel he was. Devastatingly gorgeous and strong enough to break a bus in half.

All it did was annoy me.

I scowled at him. "This can't be a coincidence."

Next to me, Claire made an intrigued noise.

I stood and stalked toward Declan, my frown deepening. "How'd you find me?"

"I'm good at finding things." He grinned. "Bounty hunter, remember?"

"That's not it."

"Fine. I followed you. Then I waited a bit to see what you'd do here."

"You were spying on me." I grabbed his arm. "Come on."

We went outside, and I dropped his arm gratefully. *Yeah, gratefully. That's it.*

"You clean up nice," he said. "But then, you looked nice covered in seaweed and squid slime, too."

I turned to him and scowled. "What are you really doing here?"

I could feel my friends watching us through the window. They were shameless.

Declan reached into his pocket and pulled out the other half of the medallion. "Need this?"

I gasped. "Damn it."

"Yeah, I thought you might."

I *really* should have stayed and looked for it.

"I saw you snag it off the ground," Declan said. "Seemed like a good idea. Except, the Seeker I gave it to last night said that he needed the other half to use it to find the demon."

"Well, you can't have it."

"No. We'll have to work together."

A stupid part of me wanted to say no immediately. And while I frequently had my not-so-bright moments, I wasn't a complete moron. Unless I tried to kill Declan and take his charm, we'd be working together. And while murdering him might have a certain appeal—and I didn't mind doing questionable things sometimes—that was way over the line.

"Fine." I scowled at him.

"One would think you're not just after the demon's blood," he said. "You seem very committed to taking him yourself."

"Of course I am. I work alone."

"Not anymore." He stuck out his hand. "You get the blood. I get the demon. Alive. Deal?"

I stuck out my hand and shook his, knowing that it was a pointless shake. I'd kill that demon first chance I got, deal or no deal. "I've got a Seeker inside. Let's do this."

He nodded, and we strode back into the coffee shop.

I smiled at my friends, trying to look normal. "We're in luck. Declan here has the other half of the medallion." I gestured to Cass. "And Cass here is our Seeker."

Yeah, she wasn't a Seeker. But there was no way I'd go ratting her out as a FireSoul. She actually had a special approval from the Order of the Magica—it was basically just permission to live, which was effed up if you asked me—but most people were terrified of FireSouls. Hated them.

I doubted Declan would be scared—he didn't seem scared of anything. But it wasn't my place to tell her secret.

Declan handed the medallion to Cass and took a seat. As Cass closed her eyes and went to work, Mari leaned toward Declan.

"So, you're the one who's been getting in my sister's way."

The corner of Declan's mouth inched up in a sexy grin. "Guilty as charged."

"Hmm." Mari pursed her lips and sat back, clearly unimpressed.

"I'm Claire." She leaned forward and stuck out her hand.

Declan shook.

Claire gripped it tight and frowned, clearly trying to figure out what kind of supernatural he was. "Fallen angel?"

He nodded.

"I've got it." Cass opened her eyes. "Or at least, I've got a bit of a clue."

I turned toward her. "And?"

"You need to go to Grimrealm."

Aaaaand shit.

Cass set the medallion on the table and shoved to her feet. "Come on, new guy. Let's go get a coffee."

She grabbed his arm and yanked him to his feet. He shot a confused look around the table, then shrugged and followed Cass to the bar. Clearly, he knew something was up, but he was willing to play along. And while this scenario wasn't ideal, Cass was right—we needed a second to talk without Declan around.

"Cass isn't the worst," Mari murmured.

High praise from her, especially when she was in her Mordaca getup.

"Yeah." She knew we were from Grimrealm and didn't like to talk about it, but that was all. We'd never shared any more with her, and had never intended to. But Cass had her own dark, shitty past, and she was intuitive. Clearly, Declan was the new guy. No one wanted to talk about the shit that scared them around the new guy.

Claire leaned forward. "I can do this, guys. Recon, and I'll report back."

"You can't," I said. "Too dangerous."

"Yeah." Mari nodded. "After that last job went south, you said you'd never go back."

"Well, I didn't have a good reason then. And you've made it your life's work not to go back."

I shuddered. She was right about that. I'd rather chew off my left leg than go back. Except, chewing off my left leg wouldn't help me catch and kill that demon.

And I *couldn't* ask Claire to go for me. Mari couldn't do it, either, though I could see from the glint in her eyes that she was raring to go.

"I'm an adult now, and good with disguises." I nodded, psyching myself up. "And Grimrealm is a big place. I don't need to go anywhere near the places we don't like." Like, near family.

"This is a bad plan," Mari said.

"It's our only plan."

"I'm going, too," Mari said.

I turned to her. "No, you need to stay out so you can rescue me if I get caught."

She gestured to Claire and Cass who stood at the register. "They can handle that."

"*No.* You know they can do worse if they catch both of us."

She paled slightly, but she got the point.

We were each other's weaknesses. We'd do anything to save the other.

"Fine." Mari scowled. "But next time, I'm going."

"Fine."

"I can lead you there, at least," Claire said. "Get you through the most dangerous protections."

I scowled at her.

"Seriously, *that* is fine," she said. "I won't even enter Grim-realm. I'll just help you get in. And trust me, you'll need my help."

She was right. I had no idea how to enter Grimrealm. When we'd been smuggled out in barrels, I hadn't seen exactly how we'd gotten out. And I'd made a point never to go back.

"Declan might know how to get there," I said. "I think he has some affiliation."

"Well, let's find out." Claire crossed her arms and leaned back in her chair.

Cass shot us a glance from the counter, and I nodded.

She and Declan returned. He held a cup of coffee and wore a slightly bemused expression.

"Looks like we're going to Grimrealm," I said. "You know how to get in?"

"No." He sat and sipped his coffee. "I track demons from Grimrealm often, but only once they leave. I've never needed to go in. So I haven't."

"Don't blame you." Claire grimaced. "It's the worst."

"You've been?"

"Yeah. And I'll lead you two in."

"Thanks." He nodded at her.

I looked at Cass. "Where exactly in Grimrealm are we going?"

"I'm not sure. I couldn't see that much."

"I have some contacts who can help you," Claire said. "But you're going to need to change your signatures so you seem like dark magic users."

I nodded. "I can handle that."

"We've got some really nasty magic back in the shop," Cass said. "I can imbue a cloak with something that'll make you stink like a fish shop dumpster on collection day."

I grinned. "No thanks. I've got a bit of dark magic. An amplification charm will do."

Cass's brows rose. "You do?"

"You had to have realized that," I said. "We live in Darklane."

"But you're not normal Darklaners," Cass said.

"Close enough." I stood. "But thank you for your help. Truly."

Mari looked at Declan. "How are you getting into Darklane?"

"Same as Aerdeca."

So he had a bit of dark magic in him as well? Interesting. I couldn't sense it. But then, no one could sense mine, either. I'd repressed it enough that it was hard to get a read on.

"Come on. Let's go." I gestured toward the door. "We have hell to sneak into."

11

An hour later, after Mari and I had whipped up a couple of amplification charms, we met Claire and Declan on our front stoop. I'd made Declan wait outside and hadn't felt even a little bit guilty.

It helped that not much seemed to bother the angel. As long as we were working together to catch the demon, he seemed happy.

Mari gave me a worried look as we walked toward the foyer. She still wore her dress and bouffant. "I hate that you're doing this."

"It's in and out." I raised my arm, which had a black cloak draped over it. "Besides, I'll have a disguise."

She shot the cloak a skeptical glance, but didn't mention anything else. I'd changed my glamour so it looked like I wore my fight suit, except I'd made it black this time. I could still use it as a ghost suit, but it'd be unforgivably dumb to wear my white disguise into Dark-lane. I'd add the cloak on for good measure, to hide my face.

I opened the door to find Declan leaning on the stair railing.

Claire strode up the sidewalk toward our place, a tense smile on her face.

"Ready?" she called.

"Can't wait."

Mari followed me out onto the step.

I looked at her. "Don't worry. I'll see you later, okay?"

She nodded, looking distinctly annoyed. "Safe hunting."

"I promise."

Mari gave me a hard hug, then went back into the house. I could feel her worry on the air.

"She really doesn't want you to go in here," Declan said.

"We're close and she worries." I handed him a tiny vial. "Drink this. It'll enhance your dark magic signature."

He nodded and swigged it back. His signature changed in an instant, going from smelling like a rainstorm to smelling like a raging forest fire.

"That's not *that* bad," I said. Most dark magic signatures smelled like rot and decay.

"Still part angel," he said. "And my fall wasn't that bad."

I definitely wanted to hear about this fall. I swigged my own amplification potion. The dark magic within me didn't grow, really. It just became more apparent. Remnants of my upbringing in the darkest parts of the world.

Some people might be bothered by it, but I'd made peace with it long ago. I chose to do good, and therefore I *was* good. Done and done.

Declan's nose twitched. "You smell like a wet dog."

I smiled. "Thanks, what a lovely compliment."

"A very attractive wet dog."

"Really? What's your preferred breed?"

He cracked a smile. "Okay, too weird."

I nodded. "Yep." I looked at Claire. "Ready?"

The cruel twist of my life was that Grimrealm actually wasn't very far from Darklane. When we'd escaped, we'd wanted to run as far as we possibly could. All the way to New York, or London.

But that wasn't the deal we'd cut with the Council of Demon Slayers.

No, they'd wanted us to protect Magic's Bend.

And Magic's Bend happened to be right on top of Grimrealm. It was the main reason we were so dedicated to our disguises. Our family didn't leave Grimrealm often that we knew of, but they had minions and friends. We weren't about to be caught by surprise one day.

We walked over to Fairlight Alley, the quiet little street that housed unexpected horrors. Claire led the way, striding down the empty alley that smelled suspiciously clean. Almost every alley in this part of town smelled of pee—there were a *lot* of bars here.

This one, however, was weirdly clean. And it was only about forty feet deep, with a brick wall on the far end.

Though there was nothing obviously wrong with the alley, I felt a strong compulsion to back away. A nearly overwhelming desire to get the hell out of there.

"Ignore the repelling charm." Claire stopped in front of the wall at the end.

I swept my cloak over my shoulders and pulled up the hood.

"Interesting choice of attire," Declan said.

"No need to be recognized." Actually, I had a distinct need *not* to be recognized. I turned to Claire, killing that conversation. "What next?"

She pressed a hand against the brick wall and pushed hard. It sank into the stone, and she stepped forward, her foot disappearing into the brick. "Follow me."

I mimicked her movements, pushing my way through the charm that made it look like there was a wall. It felt like walking through viscous goo, but I made it onto the other side.

Which was identical.

"Not what I was expecting."

"Not there yet." Claire strode forward, heading toward the end of the empty alley.

It was another dead end, just like the one we'd come through, and Declan and I joined her.

When she reached the end of the alley, she gestured to the side wall. "Stand over there."

We did as she asked, while she stood and stared at the brick wall, her head tilted. She was clearly thinking, but about *what?* She looked like a confused golden retriever staring at itself in a mirror.

Finally, she nodded as if she'd figured it out and pressed her hand to one of the bricks. Then to another, and another, going in a specific pattern that only she knew. Magic swelled on the air, and stones began to scrape against each other. In front of me, the floor opened up, a gaping square hole that belched dark magic.

I shuddered. This was *way* worse than my signature or Declan's. Hopefully we would blend down there.

Claire turned back to us, her eyes dark. She dug a tiny vial out of her pocket and popped it open, then chugged it down. She shuddered hard, and I got a whiff of rotten fish and gasoline.

I pinched my nose. "Wow, that reeks. You'll blend in well."

"I don't miss this, that's for sure." She shoved the empty vial back in her pocket. "It'll only last about thirty minutes on me, so we have to be quick. Come on."

Without another word, she jumped into the hole.

Holy fates. I'm going into Grimrealm.

My heart pounded once, hard, but I didn't waste any time. If I hesitated, I might chicken out. And I *never* chickened out.

I jumped in after her, gagging as the dark magic enveloped me. I plummeted, my stomach lodging itself in my throat. Right before I hit the bottom, magic slowed my descent. I landed easily on the ground, right next to Claire.

Oh my gods. Oh my gods. Oh my gods. I'm in Grimrealm.

I sucked in a deep breath and packed my freak-out away.

Declan appeared next to me, his dark wings flared. He folded them back into his body. Claire dragged her interested gaze from Declan and studied the tunnel in which we stood.

It was long and dark, with green-flame torches burning on the walls.

"Doesn't look any different," she said. "Hopefully the protections haven't changed."

"How long since you were here last?" Declan asked.

"A couple months." She waved us forward. "Come on."

I followed her down the narrow tunnel, keeping right in her footsteps. Claire stopped in front of a mound of earth that ran along the side. She pointed to it. "Walk on this to avoid triggering a fire trap," Claire said. "It'll barbecue you if you don't walk in the exact right place."

I nodded as if this were completely normal, but inside, I was screaming. I was in Grimrealm.

As we neared the end of the tunnel, the sound of people filtered in. Cacophonous voices, hundreds of them. A cold sweat broke out on my skin, and I adjusted my hood so it fully hid my face. I looked way different now—older, no longer gaunt with hunger—but I couldn't help myself.

The mound of dirt upon which we walked ended, and Claire stepped off.

She gestured to the exit of the tunnel. "I really can do this if you need me to."

I squeezed her hand. "No, but thank you."

"Then you'll go through there. Look for the library and speak to the librarian. She should know how to get you started."

"The librarian?" Declan sounded incredulous.

"Librarians know a lot. And a Grimrealm librarian is definitely *not* whatever you're thinking."

I could only imagine.

"And remember," Claire said. "This tunnel is a transportation zone. That means, if you want to use a transport charm to get out of here in a hurry, you have to make it back to here."

"Is it the only one in the whole place?" Declan asked.

"No, there are private ones scattered throughout Grimrealm, but you aren't likely to have access to one of those."

"Okay, we'll come back here." But we'd have to be really desperate to use a charm if we were this close to the normal exit.

Claire gave me a quick hug. "Be careful."

"I will." I squeezed her tight. My heart wouldn't stop thundering.

Claire hurried away, disappearing quickly through the tunnel.

"Let's go." I turned toward the exit and approached.

Declan stuck by my side, and though I didn't like him—at least, that was what I told myself—I did like his presence. An ally in a sea of danger and horrible memories.

Slowly, I approached the entrance to Grimrealm. The dark magic that rolled out of the place reeked so badly that my eyes watered. Like an old fishing boat full of rotting trout that had baked in the sun for a week and then had a baby with an old gym sock.

I breathed shallowly through my mouth, trying to avoid drawing too much of the stink through my nose. And the signatures *felt* awful too. Like bee stings and pinches and slimy green seaweed.

"I don't regret staying away from this place," Declan said.

"No, I agree." What would I have become if I had stayed here? If Mari and I hadn't escaped, we'd be as bad as this place.

The idea made me shudder. I'd long since come to grips with

the little bit of darkness in my soul—how *couldn't* I be dark if I'd been born and raised in Grimrealm? But I wasn't that bad.

When I reached the true entrance to Grimrealm, I stopped, taking it all in.

The famous market.

I'd never come here as a child—not really. I'd snuck away once or twice on my own, and I couldn't really count the time we'd been carried through in a barrel. But Aunt had kept a close watch on us, keeping us in our house at the far neighborhood in the back. Just the memory of it made my heart thunder.

"Your heartbeat is going wild," Declan murmured.

"This place is weird." But damn, he had good senses. I'd have to be more careful.

"I think there's a lot more to you than meets the eye."

I shot him a look. "Of course there is. I'm mystery and enigma wrapped in a riddle."

The corner of his mouth quirked up. "Your tone says you're joking, but I'd bet that's mostly true."

"Whatever." I turned to look back at the market, reminding myself that my family rarely went into Grimrealm proper, and that I was in a disguise.

We'd be quick, in and out and done in an hour.

The market was the place to be in Grimrealm, as I recalled. Hundreds of people bustled through the stalls, all of which were made of black fabric. Signs floated in the air above each stall, advertising all sorts of black-market goods. And when I said black market, I meant *black* market.

There were weapons, grimoires, shrunken heads, and potions for sale—mostly poisons from the look of them. Clothes, too, along with furniture and food. All of it had some element of black magic to it. None of it would be welcome above ground.

The ceiling was high, probably a hundred feet above us and

made of solid rock. My home was right up there, and my family didn't even realize. *I* hadn't really thought of how close they were in ages.

It was an unwelcome realization.

The market was at least two football fields in size, hundreds of stalls squished together. Bigger shops and restaurants and even a casino had been built into the walls surrounding the market. Signs were carved into the stone above the premises.

I ran my gaze over them, finally spotting a small one that said *Library*. I pointed. "There."

"Let's go." Declan took my hand, and I jumped slightly, my gaze flashing to his.

I jerked on my hand, but he didn't let go.

"We don't want to get separated now."

I scowled, but just charged forward, dragging him along. He wanted to hold hands? Fine. But he wasn't going to like it.

I was, unfortunately. My heartbeat was still going a mile a minute, but it wasn't all fear now.

I did my best to shake away the shiver that ran up my arm. I was totally not interested in him. Nope. I was only interested in finding this demon and getting the hell out of Grimrealm.

We had to weave our way through the patrons in the market, squishing between the bodies that reeked of rotten cabbage and decaying flesh. There were witches and mages and demons and shifters—all the same kinds of Magica you'd find on the surface.

Except they were evil as hell, full of dark intentions and hatred.

As we walked, my gaze roved over the goods spread out over the stall tables. Weapons and torture devices gleamed under yellow light, while potions shined like jewels in their colorful glass bottles.

I was careful not to make eye contact with anyone, though Declan wasn't so circumspect. A few angsty demons looked like they might charge him, just for the offense of meeting their gazes. But he gave them a hard look, and they backed off.

Smart demons.

Finally, we reached the edge of the market. My mind was buzzing with the few memories I had of this place, of sneaking out to try to find something happy in the world, only to return disappointed because Grimrealm freaking sucked.

By far, the worst memory was that of escaping. Of Mari and I smooshed into the barrel together, of peering out of the breathing hole while Mari hyperventilated. At the time, the thrill of possible escape had been suffocated by the fear of getting caught. That fear chilled my skin even now, worse than any I'd felt since I was a child.

Worse than falling off a cliff, facing down a horde of demons, going on a bad blind date.

Ha. As if I ever did that.

"You definitely seem nervous," Declan murmured in my ear. "You've never struck me as the nervous type."

"I'm not," I snapped, shooting him an icy glare.

He grinned. "There's the ice queen I know and love."

"Oh, come on." I yanked him forward, dragging him toward the little building that said Library over the old wooden door.

As we neared it, he loosened his grip, and I took the first opportunity to drop his hand, though I hated to admit that I missed the connection. I hurried up to the door and pressed my hand to it, pushing it open.

The air inside smelled strongly of old paper and even older magic. It sparkled with the stuff, in a way that made the air feel weird. Almost like I was in a dream. I stepped into the dim interior, taking in the tall walls stuffed full of ancient books. The leather was dusty and dry, hardly cared for at all.

Maybe it was for the best, since these books no doubt

contained darkness that should be lit aflame and burned to ashes.

"It's a maze," Declan said.

He was right. The shelves in the middle of the library left only the narrowest passages for people to use. The lights hanging from the ceiling shed a dim golden light on the space, and it was silent as the grave.

"Hello?" I called.

Silence.

"Hello?" I repeated.

"Hold on, hold on!" A cranky old voice sounded from behind one of the shelves.

A book flew off the shelf and hit me right in the head.

Pain flared and I scowled, rubbing my aching skull. "What the hell?"

Another book flew toward me, but this time, I was ready. I caught it. Three more books shot off the shelves, dust trailing behind them. They sailed right for Declan, who reached out and grabbed them.

Damn it, I really wanted my mace.

"Ugly!" hissed a voice.

"Stupid!" hissed another.

"Dumb as bricks!"

"Who the hell is talking?" Declan demanded as he deflected the books, catching them and setting them on the ground as quickly as they flew.

"I think...I think it's the books."

"Troll face!"

"Shit for brains!"

Annoyance surged through me, along with a surge of fear at being attacked while in Grimrealm. I wanted to grab my mace from the ether and smash these damned things, every one that flew at me.

"Horse butt!"

"Monkey tits!"

"Who are you calling monkey tits?" I demanded.

"You, corn ears!"

I looked at Declan as I caught a book. "What the hell is a corn ears?"

"They're not very good at insults." A book slammed into his shoulder hard enough to make him jerk. Irritation flashed on his face and he turned.

"Don't hurt the books." The voice echoed in my ears, and I swung around, looking for the source. I saw no one, though. "It's a test."

A weird test.

Declan drew his sword.

"Don't hurt the books!" I hissed. As much as I wanted to tear a few pages out—and boy, did I—we didn't need to piss off the librarian. And if this really was a test...

Declan nodded curtly, getting my gist. As fast as we could, we caught the books that flew at us and shouted insults.

Finally, when I was surrounded by a pile of dusty books that reeked of death and a cacophony of stupid insults filled the air, a figure appeared.

The old woman was dressed in an elaborate gray lace dress. She raised her hands, then brought them down in a slashing motion. "Stop!"

The books stopped flying, the insults fell quiet, with one final curse lingering on the air. "Green monkey dick!"

"That one's for you," I muttered to Declan.

He stifled a laugh. "These books have a thing for monkeys."

"I don't like monkeys," the old woman said. Her voice was high and reedy—not the one that had told me not to hurt the books.

And if I had to guess, she didn't like many things.

"So, was this a test?" I studied her dress, noticing that the lace had been intricately worked to form skulls. Appropriate.

"It was. You passed."

"Weird test," I said.

She shrugged. "I'm bored."

If this was how she greeted people, I wasn't surprised no one visited her.

"Either way, you passed," she said. "Why did you come here?"

"We need your help," Declan said.

"You can buy it."

He nodded. "All right."

She grinned, then gestured for us to follow her to the back. We trailed after her into a section of the library that looked exactly the same as the rest.

A large black cat lay curled up on a pile of books, his fur looking almost incorporeal—like it was made of smoke. Something familiar tugged in my chest as I looked at it, and its eyes flared open.

Red flame.

"That damned hellcat, here again," the old woman muttered. "Like it's waiting for something. But I can't shoo it away. They do what they want."

I let my gaze linger on the cat until the woman turned to us. I reached into my coat and pulled out the medallion that we'd glued back together. "We are looking for the owner of this."

She squinted at it and held out her hand.

I hesitated, and she grunted in annoyance. I gave it to her, loath to let go of my only clue. She raised it right up to her face and peered at it. "Never seen it before." She jerked it down. "But I'm sure my books have. They see both past and present, you know."

"*Present?*" I frowned.

"Yes. It's a living collection that knows all the goings on in Grimrealm."

Then they would know about my family. Maybe they were dead. The little fantasy made me smile.

The woman turned from us, but didn't walk away. She held out the medallion, about waist high, then commanded, "Search!"

Books flew off the shelf, this time heading right for the librarian. They passed underneath the medallion, pages flicking open and creating a breeze that blew the woman's hair back from her face. One after another, the books flew by, each pausing under the medallion to flip its pages.

It was pretty damned cool.

I glanced up at Declan, and he looked impressed as well.

Finally, one of the books stopped. The woman leaned over it, nearly pressing her nose to the page.

"Yes, yes. I see."

"See what?" I moved around to look at the page.

The old woman snapped the book shut, hiding its contents from me.

Dang it.

She gripped the book and the medallion, turning to us. "The payment, please."

"What do you want?"

"Your soul."

"Sorry, don't have one," I said. "How about cash?"

The old woman frowned. "Fine. A thousand dollars."

I looked at Declan. "Well, pay the lady."

He grinned and reached into his pocket. "Is this our first date, then?"

"No, I go Dutch."

"Quit flirting and pay up," the woman snapped.

Annoyance surged through me, at both myself and her.

Declan handed over some cash—who carried around a thousand bucks?—and she handed over the medallion. Then she opened the book and pointed to the page, where I could see an illustration of the same design as the one on the medallion.

She pointed to it. "Modern history, right here. This is a compulsion charm. It makes a demon do what you want it to do. Specific to Grimrealm."

So that's why I'd recognized it, though the memory had been fuzzy. I must have seen it as a child though never understood it.

But hope flared in my chest. "If the demon isn't wearing the charm anymore, it's no longer compelled to do whatever evil it's doing?"

Had I solved this problem already? Was I really that good?

12

"No," snapped the old woman. "Once the demon is compelled, it's compelled. Especially if the action it was commanded to do is something it likes."

My heart fell. "So a necromancy demon will be compelled to do necromancy."

"Exactly. The charm got the whole process started. He's doing it on behalf of someone—probably. But he's still doing it even if he doesn't have this charm."

Damn.

Declan leaned down to whisper in my ear, and I shivered. "Then we need to figure out who has compelled him to do this. Maybe that's our lead to him."

I nodded.

"Does it tell you who commanded him?" he asked.

"No, but The Weeds will know. He's the primary go-between for demons and those who want to hire him. Evil little bugger."

Hoo boy. If this old broad didn't like him, then he was bad. "Where do we find him?"

"It's Thursday, isn't it?"

I nodded.

"He'll be at the fight ring. Other side of Grimrealm. You'll know him by his hair. Green."

"The Weeds." Finally, I got it. "Thanks."

"Take the damned cat with you."

But the cat was already gone. A tiny twinge of disappointment surged through me, though I didn't understand it. I'd never particularly had a thing for animals. I liked them and all, just not a lot.

I took the medallion back from her, and Declan and I left quickly. Fortunately, the books left us alone on our way out.

We stepped out into Grimrealm, and the shock of it hit me once again. The library had sucked and the magic had been dark, but it'd still been removed from this place and my horrible memories here.

Declan reached for my hand once again, and I let him take it. I'd been through some seriously dark shit, and I really didn't need to hold his hand here. But I kind of wanted to.

Together, we cut back through the market, headed for the other side. I couldn't help but let my gaze run over the goods on the tables. More weapons, potions, books. It was impossible not to see them since I preferred to keep my head down while walking, to better cover my face and hair.

Finally, we reached the other side.

"This way." Declan led the way toward a narrow alley, and I kept a keen eye out for anyone I might recognize.

Honestly, most faces were a blur in my memory now. Even Aunt and Uncle. I'd worked so hard to suppress them that I couldn't recall exactly what people had looked like.

We cut through a narrow alley, the cobblestones damp beneath my feet. Since it didn't rain underground, I really didn't want to know *what* made these stones damp.

As we walked, I spotted another figure striding toward us. Tall and hulking, his gait was familiar.

A dark memory flashed in my mind. A beating.

Fear devoured me, sucking up my mind and my will. Instinctively, I called upon my ghost suit, turning invisible immediately. Even the cloak I wore disappeared, so Declan looked like he was walking alone.

Shock widened his eyes, but I didn't care. I couldn't help it.

I'd never been scared of anything—not since I'd escaped Grimrealm.

But now, I was scared.

Of this man.

His nose was squashed and his eyes a muddy brown. Confused, they searched the area where I stood, but he couldn't see me. My heart thundered so loud I could barely hear myself think.

Would the man stop? Try to talk to Declan? Try to catch me?

I'd cut his balls off and feed them to him.

The violent thought made me feel a bit better. Until the man stepped closer in our direction.

He was coming for us.

My skin chilled.

Out of nowhere, the black cat appeared. Its fur swirled like dark smoke, and its flame-red eyes were glued to the man. The cat arched its back and hissed, breathing fire like a tiny furry dragon. The flame licked at the man's legs.

He cursed and stumbled backward, muttering something about bad luck and melted skin.

Hell yeah, bad luck. It was a hellcat, and it had my back.

The man stumbled away, and slowly, my shoulders relaxed.

The cat disappeared.

Holy fates, that was weird.

"You okay?" Declan asked.

Shit.

I let the magic of my ghost suit fade and reappeared at Declan's side. "I just didn't like the look of that guy."

"So you turned invisible. Sure." He clearly didn't believe me, but at least he was smart enough not to talk about it now. "And you know that cat?"

"Never seen it before in my life." I pointed to a sign that was painted with an image of two demons boxing. "I think we're here."

"That we are." Declan entered first, and I followed, stepping into a ticket office that had seen better days. A grimy glass window protected a tiny man with big ears and black eyes.

Declan strode up to the counter. "Two."

"Fifty bucks."

Declan pulled out money and gave it to the man, who took the bills with black-tipped claws. Some kind of monster half blood for sure. I got a whiff of stinking magic as I passed him.

Two huge doors sat to the left of the ticket booth, and Declan pushed one open. The roar of a crowd surged out, and my interest piqued. Beyond the doors, there was a massive stadium. We'd entered at the top, so the whole thing had been carved into the earth below. There had to be thousands of people there, all screaming and cheering at the two demons in the ring.

They went at it, two massive beasts who smacked the hell out of each other with huge hands and sharp claws. The ground was sticky beneath my feet as I moved closer to the crowd, peering down into the arena.

Declan joined me, and we searched for green hair.

Finally, I spotted it and pointed. "There."

He was right at the front, near the ring. I found a set of stairs down and took them two at a time, counting on Declan to keep up. And if he didn't, well, that was his loss. Because I had our lead now, and with any luck, I could leave Declan in the dust.

Patrons shouted and shoved as we made our way lower, and I

took the opportunity to shove my elbow into some sides and work out some aggression. It was better than fear, after all.

I found that I definitely preferred the shops and buildings that surrounded the main market, since I'd never been in these particular places when I'd been a kid.

I reached the bottom of the ring and stopped dead when two bouncers moved to block me from going any closer. Each was at least seven feet tall and covered in muscles. Not that muscles mattered much in the magical world. I could take these two out. Or I could become invisible.

But becoming invisible was often viewed as a threat, and they might put the place on lockdown. I didn't recognize the guards from my childhood, so I called on my glamour instead. They wouldn't be able to see the white silk pants and jacket beneath my cloak, but my hair would appear to lay flat and silky instead of up in a ponytail.

Once the glamour was in place, I flicked my hood back just enough so they could see my face, but not enough that any other patrons could. I didn't know who else was in this crowd, and I wouldn't advertise myself.

"Watch out, boys. You're standing between me and my man." I gave it my best ice queen impression, the kind of chilly beauty that men seemed to like. I pointed. "He's over there."

"Tickets?" grumbled the one on the right.

"He has them." I smiled slightly, as if bestowing a gift upon him, and hoped it worked. Normally, I could pull this off in a pinch, but I was really much more comfortable with kicking ass and taking what I wanted.

It seemed to work, though, because they both parted and let me through. Maybe they were dumb enough to think a woman couldn't cause problems—which would be *really* dumb—but they hadn't looked clever. And this was the type of place where men brought arm candy.

Declan would just have to flirt his way through, too.

I cut through a row of people, headed straight for a slight guy with green hair. He looked oily and altogether unpleasant, with a pinched face that looked like he regularly stiffed the waiter.

I strode up to him without stopping, grabbing his balls before he'd even registered my appearance. "Come on, Weeds. We're going to go chat."

He made a strangled sound. "I could scream."

"You'll scream if I get my claws out, but you don't want that, now do you?" I purred.

The blood rushed from his face, making his green hair stand out even brighter. He shook his head quickly.

"Now come on." I tugged on him as I shot a glance back at the guards, noticing that Declan had gotten past them and that they also looked a shade whiter.

So he hadn't gone with the flirting method. No surprise, really.

I dragged The Weeds away from the guards, heading toward a clearing in the crowd that looked like a passageway. Declan caught up to us before we reached it.

"You don't waste time," he murmured.

"Nope." I turned right, heading down the corridor that led deeper into the back of the stadium. It looked like the kind that led toward locker rooms, and I really didn't want to see any demon balls or butts today.

Come to think of it, I'd never seen demon balls at all. And I'd do a lot to keep it that way.

Fortunately, the passage led to a darkened hallway.

"Who are you?" demanded The Weeds.

I slammed him against the wall. "You really thought it was a good idea to put the word *the* in front of your name?"

"My mother did," he blustered.

"No, she didn't. She probably named you Frank or Donnie. The Weeds is a dumb name you came up with when you were a teenager." I was guessing, but from the way his eyes widened, I wasn't far off.

I let go of his balls and looked at Declan. "You take it from here. I don't want to touch him anymore." But for good measure, I raised my hand and wiggled my fingers. "Don't forget the claws, though, Donnie."

The Weeds puffed up his chest. "You can't treat me like this."

"Of course we can." Declan pressed his hand against The Weed's throat. Not enough to choke him, but enough to make it clear who was the boss. "Now, tell us where to find a necromancer demon who was wearing this medallion."

I pulled it out of my pocket and held it up.

The Weed's eyes widened just a touch, but it was enough to indicate familiarity. "Yeah, thought you'd recognize that." I glared at him. "Now, who was wearing it?"

"No idea."

Declan tightened his hand.

"Donnie, look at me." I gestured to my face, satisfied once his watery green gaze was on me. "I'd love nothing more than to kill you. Honestly, it would make my day."

He paled slightly, no doubt believing my words. Which was easy, because they were true.

"Frankly, I'd blow this whole place up." I gestured to the ceiling like an interior decorator with big plans. "But I'll settle for tearing your balls off and feeding them to you if you don't answer my questions."

Even Declan winced a bit.

"A necromancer demon," squeaked The Weeds. "A necromancer demon was wearing it. Named Tekarth."

"What's his plan?"

"I don't know."

Declan shook him.

"The balls, Donnie. Don't forget about the balls."

"I really don't know!" He threw up his hands. "I'm just the go-between. Folks come to me; I find the demons and hook them up. Then I take my pay and go."

"So, who hired this demon?"

"I don't know that either!"

"Fates, Donnie, you're an idiot." I sighed. But he was so freaked out that I believed him. "What do you know about them?"

"Just a guy in a cloak. Had his signature hidden and everything." The Weeds frowned. "Actually, it could have been a woman."

"That tells us nothing." Declan tightened his fist.

"Wait, wait. They wanted a necromancer demon who could go into a church."

I frowned. "A church?"

Most demons could enter churches. But I had heard something about necromancer demons being barred from them. Which meant that Donnie would have had to pull some strings to find a demon who could enter one.

"Yeah, yeah. I had to find a demon who could wear a cross dipped in holy water and still not burn. It was hard, man."

Okay, to my knowledge, the demon hadn't yet been in a church. "Which church?"

"Um, Exe... Exe..." He frowned, his brow creasing. "Exeter!"

Declan glanced at me. "There's a huge cathedral in Exeter in the southeast UK."

I caught The Weed's eye. "That the place you're talking about?"

He nodded frantically.

I leaned close to his face. "Now listen closely, Donnie. You try to figure out who hired this demon."

"But they wanted to stay hidden!"

"I don't care. Figure it out. Because I'm coming back, and I'm going to want to know who they were." I gave him my coldest expression, one that I'd practiced quite a bit in the mirror when I'd been transitioning into Aerdeca, and he paled. "Be ready, Donnie."

"Hey! You there!" The voice sounded from behind, and I turned and spotted a dozen burly guards headed toward us. I shot Declan a look. "I think that's our cue."

Declan nodded sharply, then loosened his grip on The Weed's neck. We turned and sprinted, heading the opposite way of the guards.

"Get them!" shrieked The Weeds.

I looked back. "You're going to regret that, Donnie!"

He paled even further. At this point, he was basically transparent.

"Get me my info!" I turned back and ran, holding my hood up over my face despite the fact that this part of the hall was dark and abandoned.

"I have no idea how to get out of here," Declan said.

"Me neither." My lungs heaved as I ran. The guards behind us were fast, and I really wasn't in the mood to fight twelve. I'd win, but I'd definitely get a bit knocked around.

We passed a few different hallways, but none seemed to head back into the stadium where we could lose the guards, so we kept running forward.

A tiny black blur streaked ahead in front of us.

The cat!

I pointed. "Follow him."

"A cat?" Declan sounded skeptical. "All right."

We raced after the cat, which led us through a labyrinth of tunnels and hallways. Finally, we reached a staircase that went endlessly upward, and we began to climb.

My heart was about to thunder out of my chest, and at some point, the hellcat disappeared, clearly no longer interested in the aerobic exercise.

But the worst was the sound of demon footsteps, hot on our trail. They were fast, and strong, and I was running out of energy.

Finally, we burst out into the ticket booth area.

"Hell yeah." I gasped, then sprinted for the exit.

"Stop them!" shouted a deep voice from behind us.

Yeah, no way I was stopping. I raced out into the alley, then into the main Grimrealm market. The horror of it slapped me in the face anew, and I'd definitely be having nightmares tonight.

"Head for the tunnel!" Declan shouted from behind.

I sprinted through the crowd, dodging as many smelly bodies as I could. There was a commotion kicking up around us, no doubt because we were running through the market, which just screamed thief. Declan was right at my back, though, and we kept going.

A quick glance back showed the demons about ten feet behind Declan. They were so tall that their stride was enough to catch even me.

So, these were the circumstances that would lead one to use a transport charm so close to the Grimrealm exit.

"You got a charm?" I panted.

"Yeah, almost there."

I sprinted as fast as I could, pushing myself. If I were caught in Grimrealm, I might never escape. The thought was enough to give me that extra bit of juice.

Finally—freaking *finally*—we reached the tunnel. Declan dug into his pocket and hurled a transport charm to the ground in front of us. I didn't know where it was leading us—the one who threw the charm got to decide—but right now, I didn't care.

I jumped in, leaping headfirst into the ether, which sucked

me up and spun me around through space, finally spitting me out onto some soft grass.

Gasping, I stared at the sky. Until Declan landed on top of me. Somehow, he managed not to crush me.

I panted, looking up at him. "Did anyone follow?"

"No. It closed."

I closed my eyes, thumping my head back on the grass. The night was cool and dark here, quiet in the way of safe spaces. Eventually, my breathing slowed, and the panic disappeared. Along with it came awareness.

Mostly of Declan, who was still on top of me.

I opened my eyes. "You're still here."

"I like it." His dark eyes sparkled in the light.

Damn, he looked good. And smelled good. And felt good.

Warmth rushed through me, and I imagined what he'd look like with fewer clothes.

Really good.

His face was so close to mine. His lips so full.

I could just lean up and kiss him. It was a fantastic idea. My heart was going a mile a minute and my whole body felt like it was full of lava.

I should definitely kiss him.

"Aerdeca?" Mari shouted. "Are you out there?"

My head thumped back on the grass.

Shit.

I'd almost kissed Declan O'Shea.

13

Declan sighed and climbed off of me. I scrambled to my feet, brushing my legs off. Well, that had been...a thing.

I looked around. We were in my back garden. It was surprisingly big for being in the middle of the city, with a high brick wall built around the entirety.

"How did you get us back here?" I asked. "How'd you even know it was here?"

"I had to spy on you from somewhere yesterday."

Ugh. I'd almost forgotten how we were at odds here. I stalked toward Mari, who stood silhouetted in the back door, her Elvira dress sweeping the ground and revealing a spectacular amount of cleavage. It was a fantastic disguise, since absolutely no one looked at her face when she wore that dress.

I turned back to Declan, who actually wasn't looking at her tits. He was looking at my ass.

I arched a brow. "You can go now."

"No way."

"Did you have any luck?" Mari asked.

"Yes, but I need to get in touch with someone in Exeter, then we need to head there immediately." I stopped on the stoop and turned around to face Declan again.

"What are you still doing here?"

"We're a team."

"Why?"

"Because I've seen how good you are, and I don't want you swooping in and stealing my prey. If we work together, you'll get what you want—his blood—and I'll get what I want—for you not to steal him out from under me and kill him."

I scowled at him. "That doesn't work for me."

"I'm not going to ask why you're so opposed to this, but I will tell you that I have excellent contacts in Exeter who can help us out."

"Help us out, *how*?" I asked.

"I've got a guy who will know if a necromancer demon has gone in or out. With one call, we'll have eyes on the ground there."

I frowned. It was definitely too good an offer to pass up, because I didn't actually have friends over there. My closest friends were in Northern Scotland, at the Undercover Protectorate, and that was hundreds of miles away.

"Okay, come in. We'll eat while you call your buddy." I stepped back, letting him precede me into the narrow, dark foyer.

The main part of the house—our public space--was done up in a very Victorian Gothic style that suited the rest of Darklane. The wallpaper in this narrow hall was a black velvet floral print, with golden sconces on the wall. It wasn't quite my style, but I didn't hate it.

"Come on." I led him into my place, where Mari was leaning against the counter, her brows raised.

"You guys look beat," she said.

"I'm surprisingly tired." Grimrealm had done a number on me.

"You should be. You were gone ten hours."

"*Ten* hours?" I nearly shouted the words.

"Claire warned us that the librarian's place eats time. She forgot to tell you."

"No wonder I'm beat." And no wonder the librarian had looked like the crypt keeper. I walked to the counter where the tiny portal to the Chinese restaurant was located and rang the little bell three times, indicating three portions. As I waited for food, I turned to Declan. "Call your guy."

He nodded, pulling a phone out of an interior jacket pocket. As I listened to him talk, I gave Mari the rundown on what had happened in Grimrealm.

"And you didn't see anyone we know?" Mari whispered.

"No. Well, maybe. I freaked out at the sight of one big guy, but I couldn't place him." Some of my memories of the past were fuzzy, repressed by anxiety and time.

"Good," Mari said. "Then we'll just see what Declan's guy has to say."

Finally, Declan hung up the phone and turned to me. "No necromancer demon in the Exeter Cathedral yet."

"How can he be sure?" I didn't believe anything that certain.

"My guy lives there. In an apartment over the tea shop right next to it."

"Well, that's convenient," Mari said.

Declan nodded. "He's an angel."

Suddenly the story was a lot more plausible. "So, he'd know if a necromancer demon showed up."

"He would, without a doubt. He'll feel it as soon as the demon enters the city. Then he'll call us."

My shoulders relaxed just slightly.

"He said we can catch a couple hours shut-eye, and if anything changes, he'll tell us. We can transport directly there."

"I can take us," Mari said. She had the gift of teleportation, but she hadn't gotten it the easy way. It'd been one of our escape plans as kids, and she'd created the magic using our dragon blood. We hadn't realized we'd need to get to the exit tunnel to use it, though.

"We'll sleep in our clothes," Mari said. "Just in case we need to run for it in a hurry."

That was the best plan I'd heard all day. Maybe teaming up with Declan was a good idea. I'd still have to steal the demon out from under him and kill it, as he put it, but this *was* convenient.

A second later, the bell on my counter rang, and three boxes of food appeared. I went to them and opened them, then passed Mari her favorite—Mongolian beef. I looked up at Declan. "I hope you like lo mein."

He grinned. "I like everything except ambrosia."

"Ambrosia?"

"Angel food." He made a disgusted noise. "Not for me."

"Well, eat up." I handed him the container of lo mein, then dug into my sesame chicken, wondering if I should crunch up some Cheetos on top.

Nah, that was over the top. Even for me.

"Well, I'm going to hit the hay." Mari took her food and a fork to the door. "Call me on the comms charm when you want to go. I'll meet you in the foyer in a flash."

I smiled at her. "Thanks, sis."

She nodded, then gave Declan one long look before leaving.

Probably wondering where he would sleep. I was wondering that too. I blew out a breath. "I guess you can stay on my couch."

"Thanks."

I could let him sleep on the couch in our public living room

—the one in the middle house. But I didn't want him snooping around. Better to have him close.

"Come on." I grabbed a fork and ate as I walked toward the living room.

It was a narrow space, a real Victorian Darklane relic. I'd painted everything in different shades of white, with tons of textures to give it life. Blankets, pillows, three-dimensional paintings made with thick paint. There were a few splashes of color in those, but mostly, it was white.

After all the darkness in Grimrealm, I liked the brightness of the white. The calm.

I swallowed a bite of chicken and gestured to a big white couch. There were a few blankets tossed over the back. "You can sleep there."

He gave it a skeptical look. "I don't want to get it dirty."

"That's what magic is for. Don't worry about it."

He gave me a thoughtful look. "You have more at stake here than you let on."

"What?" Damn, this angel was insightful. "I have no idea what you're talking about."

He gestured around the room. "You. You're a strange one. Half the time you dress like an ice queen out of the pages of some fashion magazine, and you live in this perfect apartment, and the rest of the time you're running around half covered in blood trying to kill one of the most dangerous demons in the world. Those two things don't match up."

"Why don't they?"

"They just don't."

"That's not an answer." Even though he was right—at least about me having more at stake here. I thought the rest matched up fine. I could like pretty things and murdering demons at the same time.

"You're risking a lot for just an ingredient for your shop."

"I *like* risking a lot. Just like I like my pretty apartment and clothes. I'm an enigma wrapped in a mystery wrapped in a riddle, just like I told you, and you're never going to figure me out."

A small smile quirked up at the corner of his mouth, and heat bloomed in my belly. "I think I like that, actually."

"Yeah? Well..." I had no idea what to say next. But I knew I wanted to get him off this topic of conversation. "What about you, then? You're a good guy—I can feel it from your magic— but you're a fallen angel with some darkness. What's the deal with that?"

He shrugged, chewing and swallowing a bite of lo mein. "I was a battle angel. A high-ranking one in the demon wars."

"The demon wars?"

"Most supernaturals didn't realize it was happening because we were that good at our jobs. But there was a period of about ten years where demons were escaping hell in record numbers, in a location that was remote enough no humans saw them. I led an army of battle angels against them in a series of wars, holding them back until we finally defeated them and closed the portals."

The idea of him leading some angelic army on a hellish battlefield of death fit. He'd have done good work there, for sure.

"What happened then?" I asked.

"The wars ended. It was all I'd ever trained for. All I'd ever lived for. And afterward..."

"You didn't want to go do normal angel things."

"I didn't. And I don't think they'd have let me in, anyway." He smiled wryly. "By that point, I wasn't quite pure enough."

"All the killing?" That hardly seemed fair, since he'd been trained for that.

"And other things."

The way he'd said "other" had some heaviness to it.

"Other..." Oh, right.

He gave me a wicked smile. "I wasn't quite pure enough for heaven. So I fell."

"And now you're on earth. A bounty hunter."

"For the right causes. It's got everything I like. Danger, excitement, adventure." He gave me a long look. "And I meet interesting people. Ones that I'd like to get to know better."

Well, that wasn't going to be me. "We'd better get a few hours shut-eye so we're good to fight this demon."

He nodded. "Thanks for the place to stay. We make a good team."

"Um...night." I turned and walked away.

How the heck was I going to sleep with him so close?

"Aerdeca! Wake up!" Declan's voice cut through the deep and dreamless sleep that I'd fallen into.

Okay, that was a lie. I might have been dreaming of Cheetos.

Either way, I wasn't dreaming anymore.

I popped bolt upright, turning toward the door.

It was still closed, but Declan pounded hard on it from the other side.

"I'm coming!" I shoved my feet into my boots, glad I'd decided to sleep in my clothes, then pressed my fingers to my comms charm. "Mari, time to go."

"On it." Her voice went from groggy to alert over the course of the two words.

I bent to tie my shoelaces, then leapt up and sprinted for the door. Declan waited in the living room, and together we raced out into the main apartment.

Mari already waited in the foyer, dressed in her black fight wear with her ebony hair in a high ponytail. It was slightly poofed in the front, a mini bouffant that looked badass with the black sweep of makeup around her eyes. She wore a bow and arrow at her back. Though she could stash it in the ether like I did with my weapons, she often preferred to carry it.

She looked at Declan. "Where are we headed exactly?"

"He said the demon just arrived at the northern edge of the city and is approaching the cathedral from that direction. Somewhere in there, as close to the cathedral as you can get."

She nodded. "I know a spot. It's close."

I strode to her and took her hand. She held out her other hand for Declan, who took it. A second later, the ether swept us up in its grip, hurling us through space toward England.

Moments later, we appeared in a windy, cobblestoned street bordered on either side by ancient buildings. There was a pastry shop to my left and an old pub to my right. It was dark here, the stars sparkling in the sky above. The roads were lit with a golden glow from the street lamps, and I looked up, searching the tops of the buildings.

My eye caught on a series of spires that rose above the roofs. I pointed. "That way. We aren't far."

We took off, racing down the quiet city street, our boots silent on the cobblestones. I couldn't feel the demon yet, but he was so awful I knew that his dark magic would precede him.

A few moments later, we spilled out into a big open space in front of the cathedral. There was a lawn separating it from a row of shops on one side, and a tall blond man stood in the shadows of a narrow old building.

"That's him." Declan turned and strode toward him, holding out his hand. "Michael."

Michael shook his hand. "Declan. That was quick."

"We had good transport." He nodded to Mari and me. "These are my friends, Mordaca and Aerdeca."

Friends? That was a bit of a stretch—potential fuck buddies more like—but I didn't correct him.

I shook the angel's hand, taking in the strong signature of magic that felt like a ray of light had filled me up from the inside. He was handsome too. Almost too handsome.

I glanced at Declan.

Yep, I preferred the fallen-angel type, that was for sure. A little dark and rough around the edges.

I shook the thought away and looked back at Michael. "So you felt the demon arrive?"

Michael nodded. "Just minutes ago. I'm sensitive to dark magic such as his, and he appeared within the city walls somewhere north of here."

"Why would he choose this place?" Declan asked.

"The cathedral isn't a normal Anglican cathedral," Michael said. "It's a place of worship for supernaturals. There are a lot of them buried here. All types"

"So maybe he's looking for one," I said. "He is a necromancer, after all."

Michael grimaced. "If he tries to raise them..."

"Not good," Declan said.

Suddenly, I felt a dark prickle on the air. And the stench of dead bodies. "He's coming."

"Let's ambush him before he gets into the cathedral."

Michael pointed to the tea shop behind us. "The top floor of that shop is great for long-range attacks." He pointed to two massive bushes near the lawn. "The leaves on those bushes provide good cover too."

"I'll take the shop," Mari said.

"It's unlocked," Michael said.

"Thanks." Mari turned and slipped inside the building.

"I'll take the bush on the left." I sprinted for it, slipping inside the dense coverage. I peered out, getting a good view of the whole lawn and the streets that approached from the north. I drew a dagger, holding it lightly. Ready.

Heck yeah, this was a great hiding spot. That angel really knew his stuff.

Declan slipped inside the other bush, and Michael's white wings flared wide. He launched himself into the sky and perched himself on a roof, disappearing into the shadows.

I drew in a deep breath and worked to repress my magical signature. I frequently kept it on the down low, but I didn't want a single bit of it escaping to alert the demon to my presence.

As for the demon, either he didn't care to control his signature, or he couldn't. I'd bet the latter—he was so damned evil he couldn't wrap it all up.

A cool night breeze blew my hair back from my face as I waited. I focused on the dagger in my hand, ready to hurl it as soon as I saw the bastard.

When he stepped out from a narrow street, that same leather bag was gripped in his last remaining hand. I shifted left to get a clear view, and hurled my dagger.

It glinted under the glow of the streetlights, flying straight and true. The demon only had eyes for the cathedral, so he didn't even see it coming.

How easy is this?!

The dagger slammed into his chest.

Then turned to dust.

I nearly shrieked my indignation.

What the hell kind of magic was *that?* He hadn't had that ability before. Declan had cut his damned arm off, for fate's sake.

The demon didn't even stop walking.

A flicker of movement in the tea shop window was the only indicator of Mari. A half second later, an arrow flew through the night and smashed into the demon's back.

It turned to dust.

Crap.

A lightning bolt shot from the sky, and I'd bet good money it was from Declan. It was impossible for the demon to not notice the lightning, but all he did was grunt and keep going.

The bastard had new magic, no question.

And now he was going to be nearly impossible to beat.

As he passed me, I squinted at him, catching sight of a new pendant around his neck. It was totally different than the one that had broken earlier and led us to him.

That had to be it.

I needed to get that thing off him.

The demon was about twenty feet away from me, headed toward the cathedral. I sprinted out after him. Declan broke away from his hiding spot at the same time. Clearly, he had the same plan in mind.

The demon didn't even turn to look at us, though he must have sensed us coming.

Instead, he chucked something over his shoulder and kept walking, his long strides eating up the ground.

The package landed about ten feet in front of me, exploding in a cloud of dust that billowed twenty feet in the air.

I coughed, stumbling backward, rubbing my eyes. When my vision cleared, I caught sight of a body shambling toward me through the dust. It was gaunt and dead-looking, with decomposed flesh revealing part of its skeleton. One eye peered out of a decayed face. The other was long gone.

"Freaking zombies!"

14

I drew my mace from the ether, searching the billowing dust for other monsters. I'd never seen a magic bomb like this.

Two more staggered out of the dust, moving faster than a dead body should be able to. Which was zero miles per hour. That was how fast a dead body should move.

Declan was closest to the zombie on the left, and he drew a sword from the ether and swung it in one fast stroke aimed straight at the zombie's middle. He cut the monster in two, right as the creature reached its claws out for him.

I lunged for the one on the right, swinging my mace at his head. It crashed into the zombie's skull so hard that the head popped off. Raggedy blond hair waved in the wind as head flew like a basketball toward an invisible hoop.

Cool.

Gross, but cool. The body collapsed, but another zombie came right for me, darting in from the left. He was dressed like a farmer and looked like he'd died sometime when people thought bathing was a bad idea. He slammed his arm into my shoulder. Pain flared.

Damn he was strong.

I spun, ducking low to avoid the zombie's second blow, and swung my mace, making sure to keep the chain short. The spiked ball slammed into his middle with such momentum that it tore right through him. His top and bottom halves crashed to the grass.

Wow, fighting zombies was almost as fun as it was terrifying. They were so decayed that I could do way more damage with one strike.

More zombies appeared out of the fading dust, and I could hear someone running up from behind. I glanced back. Mari.

She pulled an arrow from the quiver at her back, nocked it, and fired. I turned to follow the projectile, watching as it slammed into the throat of one of the zombies so hard that it went straight through. Mari had chosen an arrow with particularly big quill feathers, and they cut through the rest of the neck.

The head toppled off and hit the ground.

A zombie staggered up to her from behind.

"Look out!" I shouted.

The creature swiped out a hand as she turned and hit her hard in the head. She spun away, falling to the ground. The zombie lunged toward her, but she was on her feet before I'd taken two steps to her. She drew a sword from the ether and sliced it across the zombie's neck.

A figure dived from above, a flash of white wings.

Michael.

The angel grabbed a zombie by the arm and yanked it up into the air so he could grip the leg as well. Then he yanked the creature in two. I darted left to avoid the falling body debris.

Declan was quick with his sword, beheading two zombies in swift succession. I paired off against one that had been six feet tall in real life. He was strong and fast, landing a nasty blow to my arm and leg. Had adrenaline not been racing through my veins, I'd have been limping for sure.

Soon, the battle was over, the dust settled.

I sprinted away from the body parts that were slowly disappearing. "If we hurry, we can catch him."

Mari, Declan, and Michael raced alongside me. My leg ached from the zombie's blow as I ran, but I ignored it. We cut across the lawn to the sweeping steps that led up to the cathedral.

Would he raise all the dead in the church? In the graves beyond?

Could we even fight them?

Exeter was a partially human city—if the dead started roaming around here, we'd never be able to cover it up.

I took the stairs two at a time and then shoved my way through the heavy wooden doors that led into the massive cathedral. The vaulted ceiling rose a hundred feet above me, stretching endlessly into the distance. Candles flickered high overhead, thousands of them inside massive chandeliers.

Frantic, I searched the cathedral.

"There!" Michael pointed. "The clock is different."

"Clock?" I spotted it then, a blue circle high on the side wall. It only kind of looked like a clock, with various dials and little golden dots that indicated something other than time.

Light glowed from it, projecting on the floor. Within the pool of light stood the demon. He turned to look at us, an ugly scowl creasing his face.

I ran for him, my friends at my side.

"It's an astronomical clock," Michael said as we ran, clearly never out of breath. "It's ancient, and is meant to provide information about the solar system instead of time."

Why the hell was the demon interested in an ancient astronomical clock?

As we neared, I realized that it was projecting an image onto the floor. Black with bright white dots. It had to be the solar system, or an image of stars or something.

The demon was studying it—memorizing it.

The huge blue astronomical clock was built into the wall over an old wooden door. There was a small hole cut into the bottom of the door, about eight inches across. A small black blur shot from the hole, launching itself onto the demon with a shriek.

The demon howled and lunged backward.

The black blur was a cat with smoky fur—the hellcat from Grimrealm?

No way.

But it was. Flaming red eyes flashed as the cat bit into the demon's neck. The demon roared, shaking the cat off, then ran away from the clock. The cat hurtled after him.

"I'll snap a pic of the clock's projection," Mari said.

"Thanks." We'd need that. I wanted to know what the demon knew, but there was no time to stop and study it. I picked up the pace, racing after my prey.

The two angels easily kept up with me, which was a rarity.

The demon had a good lead on us and was already disappearing through a small wooden door at the back of the church.

"The crypts," Michael said.

Of course.

I ran for the door, racing down the stone spiral staircase.

The crypt below was almost as impressive as the cathedral above. High, vaulted ceilings soared overhead, and thousands of sarcophagi dotted the space.

"Ah, shit." There were so many bodies for the demon to raise. How fast could he do it?

"It's the biggest supernatural crypt in the world," Michael said. "There's nothing in the human world to compare."

"Figures he'd come here." I searched the space, but it was so big and many of the sarcophagi were huge. They created a maze-like interior that was easy to get lost in. And the demon had definitely made himself scarce.

A moment later, Mari appeared behind us. "Whoa, this place is huge."

"Do you hear that?" Declan asked. "To the left."

I heard a faint noise from the far left corner and started toward it. Everyone followed close on my heels. A few steps later, the horrifying stench of death rolled over me. I gagged.

It reeked worse than the demon himself.

We had to be getting close.

We cut through a narrow corridor formed by massive sarcophagi. The sound of stone scraping against stone was my first warning. When the lid of a huge stone box crashed to the floor, I jumped, whirling to face it and drawing my mace from the ether.

A skeleton wearing tattered velvet robes climbed out. Jewels glinted on the ragged fabric, and a crown tilted off its head.

"I've got this one." Mari stepped forward. "Keep going."

"I've got your back," Michael said to Mari.

"Thanks, guys." I wanted the demon.

The skeleton climbed out of the sarcophagus and charged Mari, but she was fast, drawing a sword from the ether and then swinging for his head.

I hurried down the corridor, Declan at my side.

More stone scraped against stone, the lids of the sarcophagi slowly creaking open. It was the demon's doing.

We reached the end of the corridor as a dozen sarcophagi lids crashed to the ground. I caught sight of the demon standing over the most impressive burial site of all, a stone sarcophagus the size of a car. His hand glowed blue as he hovered it over the body within. The light shined brightly all around, illuminating the entire crypt in a pale blue haze.

It was the source of the awful stench.

"Behind you!" Declan called.

I turned from the demon, facing off against a dozen skeletons and bodies in different states of decomposition.

They were a distraction, providing cover while the demon did what he *really* wanted. I'd have to get rid of these guys first.

Declan was already fighting, moving swiftly through the crowd of oncoming bodies. Most were ancient—just skeletons—but they were fast and strong. The demon's death magic animated them, transferring his strength to them.

I gripped the chain of my mace and charged the skeleton closest to me. He wore a suit of armor that gleamed brightly in the blue light of the demon's magic. Black holes gaped where his eyes should have been, and his stare sent a shiver down my spine.

He charged, raising a sword high. When he neared me, he brought the blade crashing down. I darted left, avoiding his steel, and turned to face his back. I swung for his head, my mace clanging against his armor. It left a dent, but bounced off.

Holy fates, that was serious armor.

He spun, an eerily silent enemy, and swung his huge sword again. I ducked low, feeling it whoosh over my hair.

He was quick on the return, landing a nasty slice to my arm. Pain flared. The ancient blade was still sharp.

Damn, I was going to need a tetanus shot; these guys had some seriously old weapons.

Since my mace couldn't penetrate his armor, I'd have to get him out of it. I charged and slammed my shoulder into his chest with all the strength I could muster. He fell backward and crashed onto the stone floor.

I kicked the helmet off his head, revealing a partially decayed face and sweep of sandy hair. This was too close for my mace, so I stashed it in the ether and drew a sword, swiping my blade through his neck and severing his head. He lay still.

Mari and Michael had joined us and taken up the fight against the corpses. Behind me, Declan continued to fight the skeletons. He killed one, buying himself a brief second of free time. He used it to turn toward the necromancer and throw a blast of bright white flame.

Whoa.

I'd never seen fire like that.

It smashed into the demon, who howled but didn't stop his evil work.

"Heavenly fire should have killed him," Declan muttered.

Heavenly fire?

Damn. I'd only heard of it as a myth. It should burn through *anything*.

That damned charm around the demon's neck was our biggest problem. Followed shortly after by whatever he was doing to the body in the sarcophagus.

Quickly, I took stock of the battle. My three friends were holding off the skeletons well enough, along with that strange black cat who kept appearing. The small creature had leapt onto a skeleton and was trying to tear its head off—successfully.

I ducked behind a column. Though I hated to use my ghost suit around strangers, I needed it if I wanted to get close to that demon and remove his protective charm. Any hesitation was pointless now—we were at the end of the line.

We *needed* to kill that demon.

I ignited the magic in my suit, disappearing immediately.

As silently as I could, I darted toward the demon, dodging around a skeleton who didn't realize I was there. As I neared the sarcophagus, I caught sight of the body inside.

It was ancient, all the clothes decayed and the skeleton lying on bare stone.

The demon looked up as I neared, growling.

Holy fates, did he see me?

His nose twitched.

Shit, he smelled me.

His dark magic flared, another wave of noxious stink rolling off him. More stone scraped against stone.

How the hell was he raising the dead so fast while also doing something crazy with the body in the sarcophagus? He was way too powerful.

I darted toward him, staying low to the ground and keeping my eye on the charm around his neck. Movement inside the sarcophagus caught my eye, but footsteps sounding from behind me drew my attention.

I whirled, confronting half a dozen skeletons who charged right for me.

Shit, they were fast. And apparently they could sense me, even though I was invisible.

I drew my mace and swung hard for the skeleton nearest me. He wore only a velvet green robe trimmed in ratty fur, so it was easy to smash him through the middle. He collapsed in a clatter of bones.

I spun to face the others, spotting a blast of heavenly fire headed straight for the demon. It bounced off him again. His face contorted with agony and he grunted, but he was still standing. And the figure inside the coffin was rising as well.

The skeleton nearest me reached out with a bony hand, swiping for my face. I darted back and swung my mace, crushing his hand. All the while, my attention was divided between the fight for my life and the necromancer demon. All of this was about the dude in the coffin. The demon needed him for something, and he was successfully raising him from the dead while the skeletons held us off.

All around, the battle raged. We hacked our way through

skeleton after skeleton, trying to reach the demon. The corpses were fast, and some were armed. Damn the tradition of burying warriors with their weapons. It was a nightmare when a necromancer came to town. Several landed cuts to my body, but all were shallow enough that I could keep fighting. Hell, I'd have tried to keep fighting with both my legs chopped off.

I'd nearly hacked my way to the necromancer when the body that he was reanimating stood up fully. Flesh filled out its skeletal form, making it look weirdly reanimated.

He definitely wasn't totally alive again—but it was *more* alive, if that made any sense.

I expected him to step out of the coffin any minute now.

Instead, the necromancer demon raised a hand, and his claws popped out. He swiped them across the figure's neck, beheading him in one motion.

Shock lanced me.

I had *not* seen that coming.

The head toppled off, and the demon caught it. The body fell backward, useless now.

"No!" I lunged for him, sensing what was coming next.

As expected, he reached into his pocket and withdrew something. He hurled it to the ground, then stepped into the cloud of gray smoke, disappearing.

Scraping noises sounded from behind me.

"Shit." I spun in a circle, sweeping my mace in a wide motion.

I smashed two skeletons at the waist right as they all collapsed to the ground.

With the demon gone, they were no longer animated.

I stood, panting.

The hellcat was gone. Declan, Mari, and Michael all scowled, their gazes searching the crypt.

Shit, I was still invisible.

I stashed my mace in the ether and darted behind a huge column, then removed the hood of my ghost suit, fully reappearing. I stepped out from behind the column, frustration vibrating inside me. I ignored Declan's questioning gaze as I approached the sarcophagus with the now headless body.

Though it was massive and ornately decorated, there was no name. Which meant no clue.

I turned to Michael, who approached from behind. "Any idea who this guy was?"

Michael shook his head. "He's been there over a thousand years. No one knows who he was, but he was powerful. *Really* powerful."

Declan crouched down and studied the body. "Which means he probably still has magic in his bones."

Mari, who leaned against one of the huge stone columns, scowled. "We lost the demon, and he's left no clues to track." She thumped her head back against the column. "We failed."

I shook my head, my mind spinning. There was a way to fix this. There *had* to be. Hope flared in my chest. "We didn't fail." I looked at Mari. "Can you take us home? We have work to do."

She grinned. "I like that look on your face. It's your *I have a plan* expression."

I nodded, hoping it would work.

I looked at Declan, part of me wanting to ditch him here.

But I couldn't. This thing was so big—and this demon so dangerous—that I'd take any help I could get at this point. We *had* to succeed, even if that meant me hunting down Declan and the demon if the fallen angel tried to steal him.

Anyway, we were partners.

Fates, look at me, evolving. Working with someone besides Mari.

I met Declan's gaze. "You coming?"

He nodded.

"Thanks for the visit." Michael looked around at the bones

scattering the grounds. "It was a delight. Please, never come back."

Declan grimaced. "Sorry, man."

Michael shook his head. "Don't worry about it. It was the demon's fault."

"And we need to stop whatever he's doing, so come on," I said. "Let's get a move on."

Declan joined us. Mari gripped our hands, and a moment later, the ether sucked us in. We appeared in our main foyer in Darklane.

"You have a plan," Declan said.

"I do." My voice was confident, but it was partially a show. I didn't even want to contemplate failure, so I was going with confidence. "We have two new pieces of info—the picture that Mari took of the astronomical clock's projection, and the four ingredients that the demon has collected. *Four*."

"And that's special, why?" Declan asked.

"Four is a lot. It's enough that I can possibly reverse engineer whatever spell he is using. A lot of spells use the first three ingredients—Velochia blood, Merilorca root, and an obsidian athame. The athame is a bit rare, but not like the damned head."

Declan nodded. "So we'll do a spell that will determine what his end goal is. At least, what the spell is."

"Exactly." I nodded. "We know he plans to raise the dead. But when? Where? How many and to what purpose? There are all different kinds and strengths of necromancy, and this will tell us."

"And perhaps the star map indicates a location," Declan said.

"I'm going to send it out to all our friends, see if anyone recognizes it or something." Mari grinned. "Aethelred will get a real kick out of it. Maybe it will trigger a vision."

"If we're lucky." I staggered back toward the workshop while

Mari worked on sending the image out. It was a long shot, but we had *two* real clues, and I'd focus on that.

Declan joined me, wrapping an arm around my waist so it was easier to walk.

I stiffened, about to pull away, but it really *was* easier to walk like this. My legs ached from the zombie blows. And he was keeping his hand away from any of my more interesting bits.

"Thanks." I shot a glance up at him. "Heavenly fire, huh?"

He nodded. "I use it rarely, though. Too much energy."

"Yeah." I could only imagine.

The workshop was dark as I stepped in, but I had the lights on and the fire going in no time. I staggered to the shelf where I kept the healing potions and swigged one down. The aches were replaced by blissful *nothing*.

I looked at Declan. He had quite a few cuts himself. "Want one? You can save your energy by not healing yourself."

"Thanks, that'd be good."

I strode to him, walking easier now, and handed off a small vial of healing potion. I left him to drink it, my heart thundering as I moved around the room, gathering ingredients for the spell we were about to do.

"You have the power of invisibility," Declan said.

I scowled, annoyed. I'd hoped to keep that on the down low, but no such luck. "It's my suit, actually. Not me." I met his gaze. "But keep it to yourself, if you don't mind. I like being able to sneak around."

He nodded. "Sure."

I let my gaze linger on him, wondering if I trusted him.

I did, I thought.

And it was weird.

Mari joined us a moment later, her gaze roving over the collection of ingredients on the table. She got to work gathering the others.

"I sure hope this works," she muttered.

"Me too. Because I've got no other ideas." We had no other lead on him, no idea where he was or what he was doing.

"Can I help?" Declan asked.

"No thanks." I went to our bookshelf and took down a massive old leather-bound spell book.

Quickly, I flipped through the familiar pages, searching for the spell that would reveal what the four ingredients could be used for. I had it mostly memorized, but *mostly* was dangerous in spell work. This one was a spell based partially on knowledge and intuition, so Mari and I would be vital parts of it. Finally, I found the right page and consulted the list of ingredients with what we'd found on our shelves.

"We forgot the wormwood," I said.

Mari snapped her fingers. "*That* was it."

She collected it off the shelf, then returned to our stash on the table. I set the book down next to the small silver cauldron and joined her, starting to uncork the vials as she did the same. I worked my way down the ingredients list, she worked her way up, and soon, we had a cauldron bubbling with purple potion. Smoke wafted up, smelling of sage and an autumn breeze.

I looked at Mari, and she nodded.

We both stuck our right hands in the cauldron, nicking our fingers so a drop of blood fell onto the bubbling liquid. It hissed and spat, the smoke coming more fiercely. Magic filled the room, and I hovered my hand flat over the liquid. Mari laid her hand on top of mine.

Together, we fed our magic into the potion. I found every square inch of magic in my body and funneled it into my hand, envisioning pouring it into the liquid. Our hands glowed with white and black light, and I imagined the demon.

Then I began to chant. "Velochia blood, Merilorca root, an obsidian athame, and an ancient head."

Mari joined me, and I pictured each ingredient as I spoke its name. Slowly, the smoke began to curl and solidify, forming words. It would write out whichever spells used those ingredients. Because of the head, there wouldn't be many. Even the darkest magic rarely used heads.

I squinted at the letters as they curled on the air. "Time turning."

I met Mari's gaze, and she frowned. "He'll go back in time?"

"No, I think it means he can turn back time in a particular place."

The smoke twisted again, forming different words. "Reanima."

"I have no idea what that is," Mari said.

"Declan, get the small black spell book off the shelf," I said.

He was quick, following orders as the smoke twisted to form more letters. The third word was, "Oblivia Mass Incantada."

"That's a massive memory loss spell," Mari said.

I shivered. Losing my mind was one of my worst fears.

Declan flipped through the pages of the small black book and then finally stopped. He read for a few seconds, then looked up. "The head he took from Exeter was probably the first necromancer. Reanima is the most dangerous form of necromancy. It reanimates the dead—forever."

My skin chilled. "Even after the demon leaves? The dead will keep walking?"

"Walking, talking. They'll be totally independent of the necromancer—meaning they won't collapse when he disappears—but they'll follow his orders. And they're violent. They can kill with a bite."

"Oh, shit," Mari breathed.

Necromancers were terrifying because they could raise the dead. But *normally* the dead went right back to being dead as soon as the necromancer stopped doing the spell or left the area —like what had happened today in the Exeter Cathedral.

But this...

The demon could awaken every corpse in the world, if he worked at it long enough. He could go from cemetery to cemetery, creating armies of the dead. And they killed with a bite. We were screwed.

It was every shitty human zombie movie—but real.

The smoke had stopped twisting over the cauldron. There were no more possible spells.

Double shit.

He was doing the Reanima spell.

A pounding sounded at the door, and I jumped. My gaze flashed to Mari, and we sprinted toward the door.

She swung it open, and Aethelred stumbled in. The old seer had a long white beard and sported a blue velour tracksuit. Gandalf going to exercise class, basically.

And he was panting as if he'd just run miles. His wide eyes met ours. "He's doing it now. The demon. I know where he is, and he's raising the dead *right now*."

15

"Where is he?" I demanded. "And what *exactly* is he doing?"

"He's in the Darklane cemetery." He pointed out the door. "Just down the road. I saw it in the stars."

Mari's photo of the astronomical clock's projection. And he was so close to home.

"And he's just started some kind of spell," Aethelred said. "He's raising them."

"Raising them for good," Mari said. "He's doing the Reanima spell."

Aethelred gasped. "That's the bad one, isn't it?" He shook his head. "I didn't see that. Oh fates, how didn't I see that?"

"We have to go," Declan said.

I was already turning toward Mari. She held out her hand, and I gripped it. Declan took her other hand. The ether sucked us in a moment later, spitting us out at the high cemetery wall. We couldn't transport directly inside, but this would do.

"I'm calling backup," Mari whispered.

"Do it. We'll need it." I looked up at the wall. We were at the exact same place where I'd climbed in the first day I'd seen Declan.

I jumped up and grabbed the edge, then scrambled over. Declan moved just as quickly, landing at the same time I did.

The same twisting fog curled over the grass, snaking around the headstones. Yellow lamps shed a sickly glow over the scene, and I could already smell the demon's magic.

Together, we moved silently across the grass, weaving through the headstones.

"We made a deal, remember," Declan murmured.

"Yep." I remembered the deal all right. And that I would break it.

A moment later, we spotted the demon. He stood within a clearing between the graves, his arms raised to the sky. The ingredients were laid out at the compass points surrounding him, with the head pointing north.

Dark magic filled the air, prickling sharply against my skin. The stench was foul, enough to turn my stomach and make my eyes water. All around the demon, the earth rumbled. Dirt shifted as hands shot up from deep within the ground.

The dead are rising.

I spotted the charm around the demon's neck. "He's still wearing it."

"I'm trying anyway," Declan said.

I nodded. If anything had a chance of taking out the demon, it was heavenly fire. Declan raised his hand, his palm glowing white. He hurled it toward the demon, but the fire flew too low. He was going to miss.

The fire plowed into the severed head sitting at the demon's feet.

Oh, smart angel.

He didn't miss.

The head flew away, totally immolated, and I waited, breath held.

But the zombies kept rising.

Damn. The spell was already in effect. The demon no longer needed the head.

Soon, there were two dozen zombies all the way out of their graves.

"Thanks for the invite." Claire's voice sounded from beside me.

I looked over, spotting her in her fighting leathers with her sword drawn. Her left hand glowed with red flame. "You know how I hate to miss a party."

"This looks like it will be a good one." Connor grinned. Claire's brother stood next to her, a sack of potion bombs hanging over his shoulder. His messy hair was speckled with flour, and his T-shirt read *Alanis Morissette*.

"Thanks for coming." I grinned at them.

A half second later, Mari raced up, the three FireSouls at her side. The three were best friends, though they'd been together so long that they might as well have been sisters. Cass looked exactly the same as she always did since she rarely deviated from her usual uniform.

Next to her, Del Bellator was already in her Phantom form, pale blue and transparent. The dark-haired FireSoul was half Phantom, one of the most terrifying types of supernatural creatures in the world. They fed off your misery and fear.

Fortunately, Del was a pretty cool chick who had no interest in my deepest misery and fear. But she did like to fight in her Phantom form, since no one could land a blow when she went all ghosty.

Nix, the third FireSoul, grinned widely. She wore a T-shirt with a cartoon cat riding a rainbow Pop-Tart and motorcycle boots. She was a conjurer with some bad-ass life magic—totally the opposite of the necromancer, and probably really handy in a situation like this.

"Let's do this," Nix said.

We turned to face the demon, who was still chanting. Every second, another zombie rose.

We sprinted forward, heading directly toward death. I called upon my mace, hefting the chain and spiked ball.

Connor dug into his potion bag and hurled a sparkling green bomb. It smashed into a walking corpse, immediately melting its face in a blast of acid. Claire hurled firebombs, aiming directly for the heads as well. Skulls exploded, partially decayed brain matter flying through the air.

The zombies flew backward and landed hard on their backs.

Then they rose, staggering forward, headless.

"Tear them apart!" Cass shouted. Magic swirled around her, and she sprouted massive black wings from her back.

"Where the hell did you get those?" I demanded, swinging my mace at the nearest reanimated corpse and cutting him off at the middle. I'd never seen her with wings like that.

She grinned and pointed at Declan. "From the fallen angel. Always wanted to try out wings and heavenly fire."

Ah, right. She was a mirror mage, and could mimic the magic of nearby supernaturals.

Cass launched herself into the air and began to hurl blasts of white fire at the zombies, destroying them in flashes of flame. Nix leapt on top of a mausoleum and raised her hands, her magic flaring bright. It rolled over me like a cleansing breeze.

Roots began to pop up from underground and grabbed the zombies around the waist, then dragged them into the dirt.

Mari leapt onto another mausoleum and raised her bow. She fired explosive arrows at the zombies and hit them right in the middle. The arrows detonated on impact, blowing the bodies apart.

It was disgusting and cool all at once.

In the distance, a small flash of black streaked though the headstones. It leapt onto one, then bounded onto the head of a zombie. Fiery breath shot from the hellcat's mouth, lighting up the zombie's head.

Where the hell did that cat keep coming from?

"Bad-ass friends you've got," Declan said as he hurled a blast of heavenly flame at the zombie that stood between him and the demon.

"Yep." I searched the graveyard.

There were thousands of bodies here. My friends were fast and skilled, taking out the zombies almost as soon as they reached the surface. But eventually they would tire and their magic would run out. If the necromancer kept going—and he would, I was sure of it—he'd eventually overpower them with sheer numbers. Then the zombies would overrun the town.

We had to get that charm off of him, *without* getting one of his damned death punches.

I needed to find a place to focus. To do a little magic that I didn't want anyone to see—though they'd see the aftereffects. I couldn't help that, and I wouldn't worry about it now.

Quickly, I darted toward a mausoleum that would conceal me. A zombie jumped into my path—these suckers were fast— and I swung my mace for its middle.

The steel smashed right through the decayed flesh and brittle bones, but not before the bastard swiped me with his claws. Pain flared in my arm, blood soaking my suit. It turned red immediately upon contact with the fabric.

The zombie fell, but another one took its place, swiping low for my legs. I slammed my mace into its arm, then hopped out of the way of its teeth.

I did *not* want to run into those. I swung my mace for its head, crushing the skull.

All around, the battle raged. I sprinted to my hiding spot and crouched down, slicing my fingertip with my nail. White blood welled, and I raised my hand. I blew, imagining the heavy headstones around the demon rising out of the ground and slamming into him.

I'd used telekinesis before, so my aim was pretty good. The heavy marble slammed into the demon's left side. His words stuttered, and he stumbled back. A second headstone crashed into him, hitting his other shoulder.

This one took him to the ground, pinning him hard and trapping his remaining arm. I was glad Declan had chopped off one arm—it gave the demon a lot less leverage. For good measure, I sent a third tombstone at him that pinned his legs.

He roared, a sound of rage that vibrated the air around us. The zombies moved faster, a frenzy overtaking them. They were fed by his energy, and they were *pissed*.

I sprinted out from my hiding spot, determined to yank the charm off his neck. Declan was faster, though, racing toward the demon on long legs. He leapt on him, yanking at the charm. As he pulled it off, the demon got his arm free and swung a massive punch at Declan's middle.

The demon's fist smashed into him, the black light of his magic flaring. As with last time, despair overwhelmed me, his magic shooting through the air. Declan flew backward, and my heart dropped. He lay still, unmoving. That punch had been even harder than the one in the water.

"Someone guard Declan!" I screamed.

We couldn't let the zombies get to him while he was knocked out.

"On it!" Connor shouted, running toward Declan while hurling his potion bombs at any zombie who came near.

Declan had gotten the charm, so I could take out the demon.

He was currently struggling to get the heavy tombstones off of his legs.

We needed to incapacitate him further. No way I wanted to approach like this.

I caught Mari's eye from across the graveyard. She stood on top of her mausoleum on the other side of the downed demon. I raised my hand, and she nodded, understanding the signal.

I lined myself up so the demon was directly in between us and sliced my palm. Pain flared, and I grinned. Mari did the same, black blood glinting in the light.

I envisioned lightning, just like I had all those years ago when we'd created this magic. Thunder cracked in the air as lightning shot from my palm. Lightning surged from Mari's hand as well. The crackling streams of energy joined, so much more powerful because the two of us worked together.

We lowered our hands, and the lightning dropped. It hit the demon, and he roared, his body lighting up like a Christmas tree. Without his protective charm, the lightning could hurt him. Together, Mari and I fed our lightning into him. We hadn't used this power to escape Grimrealm like we'd planned—another failed attempt—but it came in handy now.

Energy poured from me, weakening my limbs and making me short of breath. Finally, the demon lay still. No way we were lucky enough to have killed him.

I dropped my hand, cutting the connection, and sprinted for him. With the way the fallen tombstones were positioned around him, the angle was all wrong for my mace. So I stashed the weapon in the ether and drew my sword, ready to take his head. He lay prone on the ground when I reached him, his face blackened and his eyes closed. Still unconscious?

I raised my sword.

Fast as a snake, his arm rose. He punched me in the leg, and the black magic flared. Pain surged through me, and I dropped to my knees, bile rising in my throat.

He was weak from our lightning, thank fates. Otherwise, I'd be unconscious—or dead—like Declan. I struggled to stay upright with my deadened leg as the demon drew his fist back for a second punch. His fiery eyes met mine, hatred blazing within.

I wanted to ask him why he was doing this insane thing, who the people were who'd hired him, but he struck out again.

I dodged left, barely avoiding his strike. With my heart pounding in my ears, I swung my blade down, aiming for his neck. My aim was true. With one clean strike, his head rolled away from his body. For good measure, I sliced off his arm and legs.

"Aerdeca! Watch out!" Someone's voice echoed across the grass, and I spun on my one good leg, searching for the threat.

Zombies still staggered across the grass, as violent and strong as ever. Freaking Reanima spell. Most magic died with the caster, but not this damned spell.

A zombie was headed right for me, claws outstretched and mouth gaping wide. I lunged for it, but I was clumsy, my leg still dead. The monster swiped its claws across my waist, and agony streaked through me, hot and fierce. I brought my blade down on the zombie's head, splitting it in two. Then I went for the waist, cutting him in half.

One by one, we took out the last of the zombies, until finally, they all lay still. All of my friends were still standing, though some were pretty bloody. All except Declan. He was still sprawled on the ground. Panting, I staggered toward him. Connor knelt at his side.

I dropped to the ground. "Is he all right?"

"I think he's alive," Connor said. "Though he's in pretty bad shape. That was some death punch."

"Bastard." I leaned over Declan, worry tugging in my chest.

"Here, he should take this." Connor handed me a small vial of potion. I didn't bother asking what it was.

I pinched Declan's jaw and poured the medicine down his throat. My friends gathered around, and the tension was thick in the air.

We waited, breath held.

Finally, Declan gasped, his eyes opening.

Relief surged through me.

Thank fates.

"Did we win?" Declan asked, his head lifted off the ground.

"Yeah, but I killed the demon."

Declan's head thumped back to the grass. "I knew you'd do that."

EPILOGUE

The next night, I sat on my front stoop. There was a chill breeze on the air, but I liked it. It was nighttime, and I'd finally gotten my hands on that martini I'd been hankering for.

Mari sat next to me, holding a Manhattan and looking longingly at an unlit cigarette.

"Don't do it," I said.

"I'm not going to." She glanced at me, her dark eye makeup sweeping across her eyes. "But I'd like to note that we face down death so much that I don't think it's going to be a cigarette that gets me."

I sipped my martini, enjoying the feel of my silk pants and top. It felt like wearing air, and was a nice change from my fight wear. "Not worth the risk."

"I suppose you're right." She broke it in half and sipped her drink.

The demon was dead and the Council was pleased, which meant that we were back to Blood Sorcery, at least for now. I, for one, had appreciated getting some decent sleep.

A small dark shadow sauntered down the road, headed straight for us.

I squinted at it. "Is that the cat that keeps showing up?"

"That random one who appeared at the cathedral and again at the graveyard?"

"Yeah. I first saw him in Grimrealm."

The cat strolled up to me, its fur partially obscured by the wisps of black smoke that drifted around him. Flame red eyes met mine. His magic smelled of brimstone, but didn't feel evil. Inherently, I knew I could trust him.

"Hey, cat," I said. "Want some tuna?"

I eat souls, thanks.

"My kind of cat." I frowned. "You can talk?"

Of course I can. The cat climbed up onto the step and sat next to me.

I looked at Mari. "Can you hear him?"

She shook her head. "He's talking to you? Does he want some tuna?"

"He prefers to eat souls."

She gave the cat an apologetic look. "Fresh out, sorry."

"What's your name, cat?"

Wally.

I looked at him, skeptical. "A hellcat named Wally?"

It's actually Wallace of Helltavia, Son of Gorgora the Dark, Devourer of Souls, and Stalker of Nightmares, but I like Wally.

"Sure, Wally." I reached out and scratched his head. His fur was hot to the touch, and a weird little tingle shot through my fingers, but Wally purred and rubbed his head against my hand. "Nice to meet you. Why are you here, by the way?"

His little shoulder moved, and it looked just like a shrug. *I like you.*

"Cool. I like you, too."

I was supposed to be a familiar to a witch down in Grimrealm but she was a real bitch. I like you better.

"So you've been shopping for a new person?"

Yep.

"Well, a little warning, then. I'm a bitch too."

Not that *kind of bitch.*

"All right then. Welcome to the team, Wally."

The three of us sat in silence a while, Mari and I sipping our drinks, and stared out at the dark street.

When a second shadow appeared on the sidewalk, approaching at a steady pace, my heart started to pound. I couldn't make out his features yet, but I recognized his walk.

Declan.

"I'm going to go get another drink." Mari stood.

I'm going to see if there's any souls in your kitchen.

Both Mari and the cat went inside—the cat was already as good a wingwoman as my sister—and I watched Declan stride down the road toward me.

He stopped in front of me. Fates, he looked good. Tall and broad shouldered, with his damned fallen angel face that had been in more than one of my daydreams lately.

"What are you doing here?" I asked.

He sat on the step that Wally had just vacated. His shoulder was inches from mine, and I swore I could feel the heat of him. A low buzz started up in my body, an awareness that prickled over my skin and made me want to kiss him.

"You really do clean up nice," he said. "But then, you always look good."

"Thanks. But that didn't answer my question."

"There's one thing I don't get, though," he said, still not answering. "You keep pulling new magic out of a hat. I've never seen a supernatural do that before. We all have certain skills, but you have a lot of random ones."

This was why I didn't like to work with a partner. Man, I really liked him. I hated that. I hadn't liked a guy in ages, and it had to be this one? He was too observant. Too smart. He already saw things I didn't want him to see, and that was dangerous.

"I told you. I'm a Blood Sorceress. Good with the charms."

"But I haven't seen any charms."

"It's not my fault you're not observant."

He smiled, a sexy half smile that made heat rise in my body. "There is one thing I'd like to observe."

"Yeah?"

"You, on a date with me."

Oh yeah, this was bad news. Because I wanted that date. And I definitely couldn't have it. Disappointment surged inside me, followed by resolve.

"Not going to happen." I turned to him. "But would you settle for a kiss?"

Interest sparked in his eyes, and he turned to me. "Settle? I don't know about settle, but—"

I cut him off, pressing my lips to his.

Heat surged through me at the first touch, and I nearly groaned. He did groan, a low rumble in his throat as he gripped my waist and pulled me toward him. His lips moved expertly on mine, and my head buzzed with pleasure.

I parted my lips, nearly vibrating with desire as we kissed. I gripped his strong shoulders and gave it everything I had. It would be the only one we'd ever have, and I wanted it to be good.

I reveled in his taste and scent, not wanting the kiss to ever end. My nerve endings lit up like it was the Fourth of July, and I wanted to throw him down on the step. To hell with being in public.

Instead, I pulled back, my breath short and my head fuzzy. I nicked my finger with my sharp thumbnail, letting the blood well.

"Forget of me, I will of thee," I murmured. Before he opened his eyes, I swiped my blood across his forehead. I repeated the chant one more time to seal it, pushing all of my magic into the spell.

He'd forget me, from beginning to end, as if I'd never been here.

My heart ached more than I expected it to, and tears pricked the backs of my eyes. I drew back to run into the house.

His eyes opened, confusion and annoyance sparking in their depths. "Did you just try to make me forget you?"

"Ummm..."

"It didn't work."

Oh, shit.

THANK YOU FOR READING!

I hope you enjoyed reading this book as much as I enjoyed writing it. Reviews are *so* helpful to authors. I really appreciate all reviews, both positive and negative. If you want to leave one, you can do so on Amazon or GoodReads.

If you'd like to learn a little more about the FireSouls, you can join my mailing list to get a free copy of *Hidden Magic*, a story of their early adventures. Turn the page for an excerpt.

The next book in Aeri's series will be coming within the month, so keep an eye out.

EXCERPT OF HIDDEN MAGIC

Jungle, Southeast Asia
Five years before the events in Ancient Magic

"How much are we being paid for this job again?" I glanced at the dudes filling the bar. It was a motley crowd of supernaturals, many of whom looked shifty as hell.

"Not nearly enough for one as dangerous as this." Del frowned at the man across the bar, who was giving her his best sexy face. There was a lot of eyebrow movement happening. "Is he having a seizure?"

"Looks like it." Nix grinned. "Though I gotta say, I wasn't expecting this. We're basically in a tree, for magic's sake. In the middle of the jungle! Where are all these dudes coming from?"

"According to my info, there's a mining operation near here. Though I'd say we're more *under* a tree than *in* a tree."

"I'm with Cass," Del said. "Under, not in."

"Fair enough," Nix said.

We were deep in Southeast Asia, in a bar that had long ago been reclaimed by the jungle. A massive fig tree had grown over and around the ancient building, its huge roots strangling the stone walls. It was straight out of a fairy tale.

Monks had once lived here, but a few supernaturals of indeterminate species had gotten ahold of it and turned it into a watering hole for the local supernaturals. We were meeting our contact here, but he was late.

"Hey, pretty lady." A smarmy voice sounded from my left. "What are you?"

I turned to face the guy who was giving me the up and down, his gaze roving from my tank top to my shorts. He wasn't Clarence, our local contact. And if he meant "what kind of supernatural are you?" I sure as hell wouldn't be answering. That could get me killed.

"Not interested is what I am," I said.

"Aww, that's no way to treat a guy." He grabbed my hip, rubbed his thumb up and down.

I smacked his hand away, tempted to throat-punch him. It was my favorite move, but I didn't want to start a fight before Clarence got here. Didn't want to piss off our boss.

The man raised his hands. "Hey, hey. No need to get feisty. You three sisters?"

I glanced at Nix and Del, at their dark hair that was so different from my red. We were all about twenty, but we looked nothing alike. And while we might call ourselves sisters—*deirfiúr* in our native Irish—this idiot didn't know that.

"Go away." I had no patience for dirt bags who touched me without asking. "Run along and flirt with your hand, because that's all the action you'll be getting tonight."

His face turned a mottled red, and he raised a fist. His magic welled, the scent of rotten fruit overwhelming.

He thought he was going to smack me? Or use his magic against me?

Ha.

I lashed out, punching him in the throat. His eyes bulged and he gagged. I kneed him in the crotch, grinning when he keeled over.

"Hey!" A burly man with a beard lunged for us, his buddy beside him following. "That's no way—"

"To treat a guy?" I finished for him as I kicked out at him. My tall, heavy boots collided with his chest, sending him flying backward. I never used my magic—didn't want to go to jail and didn't want to blow things up—but I sure as hell could fight.

His friend raised his hand and sent a blast of wind at us. It threw me backward, sending me skidding across the floor.

By the time I'd scrambled to my feet, a brawl had broken out in the bar. Fists flew left and right, with a bit of magic thrown in. Nothing bad enough to ruin the bar, like jets of flame, because no one wanted to destroy the only watering hole for a hundred miles, but enough that it lit up the air with varying magical signatures.

Nix conjured a baseball bat and swung it at a burly guy who charged her, while Del teleported behind a horned demon and smashed a chair over his head. I'd always been jealous of Del's ability to sneak up on people like that.

All in all, it was turning into a good evening. A fight between supernaturals was fun.

"Enough!" the bartender bellowed. "Or no more beer!"

The patrons quieted immediately. Fights might be fun, but they weren't worth losing beer over.

I glared at the jerk who'd started it. There was no way I'd take the blame, even though I'd thrown the first punch. He should have known better.

The bartender gave me a look and I shrugged, hiking a thumb at the jerk who'd touched me. "He shoulda kept his hands to himself."

"Fair enough," the bartender said.

I nodded and turned to find Nix and Del. They'd grabbed our beers and were putting them on a table in the corner. I went to join them.

We were a team. Sisters by choice, ever since we'd woken in a field at fifteen with no memories other than those that said we were FireSouls on the run from someone who had hurt us. Who was hunting us.

Our biggest goal, even bigger than getting out from under our current boss's thumb, was to save enough money to buy concealment charms that would hide us from the monster who hunted us. He was just a shadowy memory, but it was enough to keep us running.

"Where is Clarence, anyway?" I pulled my damp tank top away from my sweaty skin. The jungle was damned hot. We couldn't break into the temple until Clarence gave us the information we needed to get past the guard at the front. And we didn't need to spend too much longer in this bar.

Del glanced at her watch, her blue eyes flashing with annoyance. "He's twenty minutes late. Old Man Bastard said he should be here at eight."

Old Man Bastard—OMB for short—was our boss. His name said it all. Del, Nix, and I were FireSouls, the most despised species of supernatural because we could steal other magical being's powers if we killed them. We'd never done that, of course, but OMB didn't care. He'd figured out our secret when we were too young to hide it effectively and had been blackmailing us to work for him ever since.

It'd been four years of finding and stealing treasure on his behalf. Treasure hunting was our other talent, a gift from the dragon with whom legend said we shared a soul. No one had seen a dragon in centuries, so I wasn't sure if the legend was even true, but dragons were covetous, so it made sense they had a knack for finding treasure.

"What are we after again?" Nix asked.

"A pair of obsidian daggers," Del said. "Nice ones."

"And how much is this job worth?" Nix repeated my earlier question. Money was always on our minds. It was our only chance at buying our freedom, but OMB didn't pay us enough for it to be feasible anytime soon. We kept meticulous track of our earnings and saved like misers anyway.

"A thousand each."

"Damn, that's pathetic." I slouched back in my chair and stared up at the ceiling, too bummed about our crappy pay to even be impressed by the stonework and vines above my head.

"Hey, pretty ladies." The oily voice made my skin crawl. We just couldn't get a break in here. I looked up to see Clarence, our contact.

Clarence was a tall man, slender as a vine, and had the slicked back hair and pencil-thin mustache of a 1940s movie star. Unfortunately, it didn't work on him. Probably because his stare was like a lizard's. He was more Gomez Addams than Clark Gable. I'd bet anything that he liked working for OMB.

"Hey, Clarence," I said. "Pull up a seat and tell us how to get into the temple."

Clarence slid into a chair, his movement eerily snakelike. I shivered and scooted my chair away, bumping into Del. The scent of her magic flared, a clean hit of fresh laundry, as she no doubt suppressed her instinct to transport away from Clarence. If I had her gift of teleportation, I'd have to repress it as well.

"How about a drink first?" Clarence said.

Del growled, but Nix interjected, her voice almost nice. She had the most self control out of the three of us. "No can do, Clarence. You know... Mr. Oribis"—her voice tripped on the name, probably because she wanted to call him OMB—"wants the daggers soon. Maybe next time, though."

"Next time." Clarence shook his head like he didn't believe

her. He might be a snake, but he was a clever one. His chest puffed up a bit. "You know I'm the only one who knows how to get into the temple. How to get into any of the places in this jungle."

"And we're so grateful you're meeting with us. Mr. Oribis is so grateful." Nix dug into her pocket and pulled out the crumpled envelope that contained Clarence's pay. We'd counted it and found—unsurprisingly—that it was more than ours combined, even though all he had to do was chat with us for two minutes. I'd wanted to scream when I'd seen it.

Clarence's gaze snapped to the money. "All right, all right."

Apparently his need to be flattered went out the window when cash was in front of his face. Couldn't blame him, though. I was the same way.

"So, what are we up against?" I asked.

The temple containing the daggers had been built by supernaturals over a thousand years ago. Like other temples of its kind, it was magically protected. Clarence's intel would save us a ton of time and damage to the temple if we could get around the enchantments rather than breaking through them.

"Dvarapala. A big one."

"A gatekeeper?" I'd seen one of the giant, stone monster statues at another temple before.

"Yep." He nodded slowly. "Impossible to get through. The temple's as big as the Titanic—hidden from humans, of course —but no one's been inside in centuries, they say."

Hidden from humans was a given. They had no idea supernaturals existed, and we wanted to keep it that way.

"So how'd you figure out the way in?" Del asked. "And why *haven't* you gone in? Bet there's lots of stuff you could fence in there. Temples are usually full of treasure."

"A bit of pertinent research told me how to get in. And I'd

rather sell the entrance information and save my hide. It won't be easy to get past the booby traps in there."

Hide? Snakeskin, more like. Though he had a point. I didn't think he'd last long trying to get through a temple on his own.

"So? Spill it," I said, anxious to get going.

He leaned in, and the overpowering scent of cologne and sweat hit me. I grimaced, held my breath, then leaned forward to hear his whispers.

As soon as Clarence walked away, the communications charms around my neck vibrated. I jumped, then groaned. Only one person had access to this charm.

I shoved the small package Clarence had given me into my short's pocket and pressed my fingertips to the comms charm, igniting its magic.

"Hello, Mr. Oribis." I swallowed my bile at having to be polite.

"Girls," he grumbled.

Nix made a gagging face. We hated when he called us girls.

"Change of plans. You need to go to the temple tonight."

"What? But it's dark. We're going tomorrow." He never changed the plans on us. This was weird.

"I need the daggers sooner. Go tonight."

My mind raced. "The jungle is more dangerous in the dark. We'll do it if you pay us more."

"Twice the usual," Del said.

A tinny laugh echoed from the charm. "Pay *you* more? You're lucky I pay you at all."

I gritted my teeth and said, "But we've been working for you for four years without a raise."

"And you'll be working for me for four more years. And four

after that. And four after that." Annoyance lurked in his tone. So did his low opinion of us.

Del's and Nix's brows crinkled in distress. We'd always suspected that OMB wasn't planning to let us buy our freedom, but he'd dangled that carrot in front of us. What he'd just said made that seem like a big fat lie, though. One we could add to the many others he'd told us.

An urge to rebel, to stand up to the bully who controlled our lives, seethed in my chest.

"No," I said. "You treat us like crap, and I'm sick of it. Pay us fairly."

"I treat you like *crap,* as you so eloquently put it, because that is exactly what you are. *FireSouls.*" He spit the last word, imbuing it with so much venom I thought it might poison me.

I flinched, frantically glancing around to see if anyone in the bar had heard what he'd called us. Fortunately, they were all distracted. That didn't stop my heart from thundering in my ears as rage replaced the fear. I opened my mouth to shout at him, but snapped it shut. I was too afraid of pissing him off.

"Get it by dawn," he barked. "Or I'm turning one of you in to the Order of the Magica. Prison will be the least of your worries. They might just execute you."

I gasped. "You wouldn't." Our government hunted and imprisoned—or destroyed—FireSouls.

"Oh, I would. And I'd enjoy it. The three of you have been more trouble than you're worth. You're getting cocky, thinking you have a say in things like this. Get the daggers by dawn, or one of you ends up in the hands of the Order."

My skin chilled, and the floor felt like it had dropped out from under me. He was serious.

"Fine." I bit off the end of the word, barely keeping my voice from shaking. "We'll do it tonight. Del will transport them to you as soon as we have them."

"Excellent." Satisfaction rang in his tone, and my skin crawled. "Don't disappoint me, or you know what will happen."

The magic in the charm died. He'd broken the connection.

I collapsed back against the chair. In times like these, I wished I had it in me to kill. Sure, I offed demons when they came at me on our jobs, but that was easy because they didn't actually die. Killing their earthly bodies just sent them back to their hell.

But I couldn't kill another supernatural. Not even OMB. It might get us out of this lifetime of servitude, but I didn't have it in me. And what if I failed? I was too afraid of his rage—and the consequences—if I didn't succeed.

"Shit, shit, shit." Nix's green eyes were stark in her pale face. "He means it."

"Yeah." Del's voice shook. "We need to get those daggers."

"Now," I said.

"I wish I could just conjure a forgery," Nix said. "I really don't want to go out into the jungle tonight. Getting past the Dvarapala in the dark will suck."

Nix was a conjurer, able to create almost anything using just her magic. Massive or complex things, like airplanes or guns, were outside of her ability, but a couple of daggers wouldn't be hard.

Trouble was, they were a magical artifact, enchanted with the ability to return to whoever had thrown them. Like boomerangs. Though Nix could conjure the daggers, we couldn't enchant them.

"We need to go. We only have six hours until dawn." I grabbed my short swords from the table and stood, shoving them into the holsters strapped to my back.

A hush descended over the crowded bar.

I stiffened, but the sound of the staticky TV in the corner made me relax. They weren't interested in me. Just the news, which was probably being routed through a dozen techno-witches to get this far into the jungle.

The grave voice of the female reporter echoed through the quiet bar. "The FireSoul was apprehended outside of his apartment in Magic's Bend, Oregon. He is currently in the custody of the Order of the Magica, and his trial is scheduled for tomorrow morning. My sources report that execution is possible."

I stifled a crazed laugh. Perfect timing. Just what we needed to hear after OMB's threat. A reminder of what would happen if he turned us into the Order of the Magica. The hush that had descended over the previously rowdy crowd—the kind of hush you get at the scene of a big accident—indicated what an interesting freaking topic this was. FireSouls were the bogeymen. *I* was the bogeyman, even though I didn't use my powers. But as long as no one found out, we were safe.

My gaze darted to Del and Nix. They nodded toward the door. It was definitely time to go.

As the newscaster turned her report toward something more boring and the crowd got rowdy again, we threaded our way between the tiny tables and chairs.

I shoved the heavy wooden door open and sucked in a breath of sticky jungle air, relieved to be out of the bar. Night creatures screeched, and moonlight filtered through the trees above. The jungle would be a nice place if it weren't full of things that wanted to kill us.

"We're never escaping him, are we?" Nix said softly.

"We will." Somehow. Someday. "Let's just deal with this for now."

We found our motorcycles, which were parked in the lot with a dozen other identical ones. They were hulking beasts with massive, all-terrain tires meant for the jungle floor. We'd done a lot of work in Southeast Asia this year, and these were our favored forms of transportation in this part of the world.

Del could transport us, but it was better if she saved her power. It wasn't infinite, though it did regenerate. But we'd learned a long time ago to save Del's power for our escape. Nothing worse than being trapped in a temple with pissed off guardians and a few tripped booby traps.

We'd scouted out the location of the temple earlier that day, so we knew where to go.

I swung my leg over Secretariat—I liked to name my vehicles—and kicked the clutch. The engine roared to life. Nix and Del followed, and we peeled out of the lot, leaving the dingy yellow light of the bar behind.

Our headlights illuminated the dirt road as we sped through the night. Huge fig trees dotted the path on either side, their twisted trunks and roots forming an eerie corridor. Elephant-ear sized leaves swayed in the wind, a dark emerald that gleamed in the light.

Jungle animals howled, and enormous lightning bugs flitted along the path. They were too big to be regular bugs, so they were most likely some kind of fairy, but I wasn't going to stop to investigate. There were dangerous creatures in the jungle at night—one of the reasons we hadn't wanted to go now—and in our world, fairies could be considered dangerous.

Especially if you called them lightning bugs.

A roar sounded in the distance, echoing through the jungle and making the leaves rustle on either side as small animals scurried for safety.

The roar came again, only closer.

Then another, and another.

"Oh shit," I muttered. This was bad.

~~~

Click here to join my mailing list and get a free copy of *Hidden Magic*.

AUTHOR'S NOTE

Thank you for reading *Demon Slayer!* If you have read any of my other books, you might be familiar with the fact that I like to include historical places and mythological elements. I always discuss them in the author's note. But first, I'd like to talk a little bit more about the dedication of this book.

This book is dedicated to A.J., the son of my dear friend and fellow author, Kimberly Loth. The world lost A.J. too soon to depression, a disease, like cancer or diabetes, that affects millions. Depression too often goes untreated because of social stigma, but if you or someone you love is suffering with depression, please seek professional help. One option is the Suicide Prevention Lifeline at https://suicidepreventionlifeline.org/

As for the historical places in this particular book, the main one is Exeter Cathedral. The astronomical clock in the book is based on the same astronomical clock that is located in the cathedral. It dates from around 1484 A.D. and shows the hour of the day, as well as the day of the month and the phase of the moon.

There is a wooden door beneath the clock into which a hole has been cut. Historians believe that the hole may have been made to permit the cathedral cat to pass through easily so that he or she could more effectively hunt the mice that were attracted to the animal fat that was used to grease the clock. When I read this, I knew that Wally the hellcat had to come bolting out of there. It is possible that the children's song Hickory Dickory Dock was inspired by this clock.

The enormous crypt beneath Exeter Cathedral was a product of my imagination. There is no huge crypt below the cathedral. However, the front lawn (upon which Aeri and her friends fight zombies) is overfilled with ancient bones. What is now a picnic site was once an ancient burial ground into which all the dead in Exeter were interred. Throughout the Middle Ages, if you died within the walls of Exeter city, you were buried on the church grounds—no exceptions. There are an estimated 50,000-100,000 bodies buried in the yard outside of the cathedral.

And one final, fun little thing. The tea shop where Mari shot her arrows is a real place called Tea on the Green and it has a great view of the Cathedral.

I think that's it for the history and mythology in *Demon Slayer*—at least the big things. I hope you enjoyed the book and will come back for more of the FireSouls and Dragon Gods's worlds.

ACKNOWLEDGMENTS

Thank you, Ben, for everything. There would be no books without you.

Thank you to Jena O'Connor and Lindsey Loucks for your excellent editing. The book is immensely better because of you!

Thank you to Orina Kafe for the beautiful cover art.

ABOUT LINSEY

Before becoming a writer, Linsey Hall was a nautical archaeologist who studied shipwrecks from Hawaii and the Yukon to the UK and the Mediterranean. She credits fantasy and historical romances with her love of history and her career as an archaeologist. After a decade of tromping around the globe in search of old bits of stuff that people left lying about, she settled down and started penning her own romance novels. Her Dragon's Gift series draws upon her love of history and the paranormal elements that she can't help but include.

COPYRIGHT